Praise for *Rainwater* by Sandra Brown

"A quiet, character-driven piece that tugs at the heartstrings. . . .
Brown's inspiration for *Rainwater* came from her grandfather's experiences during the 1930s, and it shows. *Rainwater* has a deeply
personal feel to it, and there's a careful, loving tone that carries
through in its simplicity. . . . A beautiful little tale with an engaging, timeless feel."

—*Deseret News* (Salt Lake City)

"Bestseller Brown brings Depression-era Texas to vivid life in this
poignant short novel. . . . A contemporary frame adds a neat twist
to this heartwarming but never cloying historical."

—*Publishers Weekly* (starred review)

"Brown's characters are so real they haunt you after reading."

—*Winnipeg Free Press* (Canada)

"Gentle. . . . many will be irresistibly drawn in by this mesmer-
izing little fable."

—*Booklist*

"This beautifully written period piece transports us to 1934
Depression-era Texas. . . . A parable perfect to showcase Sandra
Brown's newly displayed brilliance as a skilled lyricist as well as
storyteller."

—*Providence Journal-Bulletin* (RI)

"Part historical novel, part tender love story. . . . Readers . . . will
be caught up as the story intensifies and races to a startling ending. A great book."

—*Minneapolis Star Tribune*

Rainwater is also available as an eBook

SANDRA BROWN

RAINWATER

SIMON & SCHUSTER PAPERBACKS

New York   London   Toronto   Sydney   New Delhi

Simon & Schuster
1230 Avenue of the Americas
New York, NY 10020

First Simon & Schuster trade paperback edition December 2018

SIMON & SCHUSTER and colophon are registered trademarks of Simon & Schuster, Inc.

For information about special discounts for bulk purchases, please contact Simon & Schuster Special Sales at 1-866-506-1949 or business@simonandschuster.com

The Simon & Schuster Speakers Bureau can bring authors to your live event. For more information or to book an event contact the Simon & Schuster Speakers Bureau at 1-866-248-3049 or visit our website at www.simonspeakers.com.

Manufactured in the United States of America

10 9 8 7 6 5 4 3 2 1

ISBN 978-1-4391-7277-3
ISBN 978-1-5011-9967-7 (pbk)
ISBN 978-1-4391-7613-9 (ebook)

To Daddy who inspired the story,
and to Mop who inspired me.

ACKNOWLEDGMENTS

I wrote *Rainwater* between two books under contract. I worked on it when I had the time, and became homesick for it when I didn't. None of my business associates knew that I was writing it until it was finished. Because it is so different from what I've been writing for the past twenty years, I submitted it with a great deal of trepidation, unsure how it would be received.

For their enormously gratifying response to the story and the possibilities it represented, I have these people to thank: *Rainwater*'s first reader, my husband Michael Brown; my agent Maria Carvainis; my editor Marysue Rucci; publishers Carolyn Reidy, David Rosenthal, and Louise Burke; associate publisher Aileen Boyle; publicity director Tracey Guest; and all the other personnel at Simon & Schuster and Pocket Books who have put their energy and enthusiasm into seeing this book published.

—Sandra Brown

PROLOGUE

"By any chance, is your pocket watch for sale?"

The old man raised his head. The woman asking about his watch was leaning across the glass display case separating them. Inside the case were snuffboxes, hatpins, razors with bone handles, saltcellars with their dainty sterling silver spoons, and various pieces of jewelry recently acquired at an estate sale.

But the woman's focus was on his watch.

He guessed the woman and her husband to be in their mid-forties. To them the gold timepiece probably looked dapper and quaint, Rockwellian. The couple were dressed in the preppy fashion of country club members. Both were trim and tanned, and they looked good together, as though they had come as a set, the man as handsome as his wife was attractive.

They had arrived in a sleek SUV, which looked out of place on the dusty gravel parking lot in front of the antiques store. In the half hour they'd been there, several items in his inventory had attracted their interest. The things they had decided to purchase were of good quality. As their appearances indicated, they had discriminating taste.

The old man had been listing the items on a sales receipt when his customer posed the question about his pocket watch. He laid a protective hand over it where it rested against his vest and smiled. "No, ma'am. I couldn't part with my watch."

She had the confidence of a pretty woman who was accustomed to beguiling people with her smile. "Not for any price? You don't see pocket watches like that these days. The new ones look . . . well, new. Shininess makes them appear phony and cheap, doesn't it? A patina, like that on yours, gives it character."

Her husband, who'd been browsing the bookshelves, joined them at the counter. Like his wife, he leaned across the display case to better inspect the watch's workmanship. "Twenty-four-karat gold?"

"I would imagine so, although I've never had it appraised."

"I'd take it without having it appraised," the man said.

"I wouldn't consider selling it. Sorry." The shopkeeper bent over the case and continued to painstakingly write up their purchases. Some days the arthritis in his knuckles made handwriting difficult, but what place did a computer have in an antiques store? Besides, he distrusted them.

He did the arithmetic the old-fashioned way, carrying over the two and arriving at his total. "With tax, it comes to three hundred sixty-seven dollars and forty-one cents."

"Sounds fair enough." The man pinched a credit card out of a small alligator wallet and slid it across the top of the case. "Add two bottles of Evian, please." He went to the sleek refrigerated cabinet with a glass door. It had no place in an antiques store, either, but thirsty browsers stayed to browse longer if drinks were available, so the refrigerator was the shopkeeper's one small concession to modernity.

"On the house," he told his customer. "Help yourself."

"That's awfully nice of you."

"I can afford it," he told them with a smile. "This is my biggest single sale of the weekend."

The man took two bottles of water from the refrigerator and passed one to his wife, then signed the credit card receipt. "Do you get a lot of traffic off the interstate?"

The store owner nodded. "People who're in no particular hurry to get where they're going."

"We noticed your billboard," the woman said. "It caught our attention, and, on the spur of the moment, we decided to take the exit."

"The rental on that billboard is expensive as all get-out. I'm glad to know it's working." He began carefully wrapping their purchases in sheets of tissue paper.

The man took a look around the shop, glanced out at the parking lot, which was empty except for his own gas guzzler, and asked, somewhat doubtfully, "Do you do a good business?"

"Fair to middling. The store's more a hobby than anything. It keeps me active, keeps my mind sharp. Gives me something to do in my retirement."

"What line of work were you in?"

"Textiles."

"Were antiques always an interest?" the woman asked.

"No," he admitted sheepishly. "Like most things in life, this"—he raised his hands to indicate the shop—"came about unexpectedly."

The lady pulled forward a tall stool and sat down. "It sounds like there's a story."

The old man smiled, welcoming her interest and the opportunity to chat. "The furnishings from my mother's house had been in storage for years. When I retired and had time to sort through everything, I realized I didn't have any use for most of the stuff, but I thought other people might. So I started selling off china and doodads. Gradual like, at weekend flea markets and such. I wasn't all that ambitious, but, as it turned out, I was a pretty good merchant.

"Soon friends and acquaintances began bringing me items to sell on consignment. Almost before I knew it, I'd run out of space in the garage and had to rent this building."

He shook his head, chuckling. "I just sort of fell into becoming an antiques dealer. But I like it." He grinned at them. "Keeps me occupied, keeps me in spending money, and I get to meet nice folks like y'all. Where's your home?"

They told him they were from Tulsa and had been to San Antonio for a long golf weekend with friends. "We're not on a deadline to get home, so when we saw your sign, we decided to stop and take a look. We're furnishing our lake house with antiques and rustics."

"I'm glad you stopped." He passed the woman a business card with the shop's logo on it. "If you change your mind about that Spode tureen you spent so much time considering, call me. I ship."

"I just might." She ran her finger over the name embossed on the card as she read it aloud. "Solly's. That's an unusual name. First or last?"

"First. Short for Solomon, after the wise king in the Old Testament." He smiled ruefully. "I've often wondered if my mother had second thoughts about that choice."

"That's twice you've mentioned your mother." The woman's smile was warmer, even prettier, when she wasn't using it to try to finagle her way. "You must have been very close to her. I mean, I assume she's no longer living."

"She died in the late sixties." He reflected on how long ago that must sound to this couple. They would have been babies. "Mother and I were very close. I miss her to this day. She was a lovely woman."

"Is Gilead your home?"

"I was born here, in a big yellow house that had belonged to my maternal grandparents."

"Do you have a family?"

"My wife passed on eight years ago. I have two children, a boy and a girl. Both live in Austin. Between them, they've given me six grandchildren, the oldest of which is about to get married."

"We have two sons," the woman said. "Both are students at Oklahoma State."

"Children are a joy."

The woman laughed. "As well as a challenge."

Her husband had been following their conversation while examining the selections in the bookcase. "These are first editions."

"All signed and in excellent condition," the shopkeeper said. "I picked them up at an estate sale not long ago."

"Impressive collection." The man ran his finger along the row of book spines. "Truman Capote's *In Cold Blood*. A Steinbeck. Norman Mailer. Thomas Wolfe." He turned to the merchant and grinned. "I should have left my credit card out."

"I also take cash."

The customer laughed. "I'll bet you do."

His wife added, "For everything except your pocket watch."

The old man slipped the fob through the buttonhole on his vest and cupped the watch in his palm. It hadn't lost a second since he'd last wound it. Time had yellowed the white face, but the slight discoloration gave it a richer look. The black hands were as thin as the filaments of a spider's web. The long hand had a sharp arrow point. "I wouldn't take anything for it, ma'am."

Softly she said, "It's invaluable to you."

"In the strictest sense."

"How old is it?" the man asked.

"I don't know for certain," replied the shopkeeper, "but its age isn't what makes it meaningful to me." He turned it facedown and extended his hand to them so they could read the inscription on the back of the gold case.

"August eleventh, 1934," the woman read aloud. Then looking back at him, she asked, "What does it commemorate? An anniversary? Birthday? Something exceptional?"

"Exceptional?" The old man smiled. "Not particularly. Just very special."

ONE

When Ella Barron woke up that morning, she didn't expect it to be a momentous day.

Her sleep hadn't been interrupted by a subconscious premonition. There had been no change in the weather, no sudden shift in the atmosphere, no unusual sound to startle her awake.

As on most mornings, sleep released her gradually a half hour before daylight. She yawned and stretched, her feet seeking cool spots between the sheets. But catching another forty winks was out of the question. To indulge in such a luxury would never have crossed her mind. She had responsibilities, chores that couldn't be shirked or even postponed. She lay in bed only long enough to remember what day of the week it was. Wash day.

She quickly made her bed, then checked on Solly, who was still deep in slumber.

She dressed with customary efficiency. With no time for vanity, she hastily twisted her long hair into a bun on the back of her head and secured it with pins, then left her bedroom and made her way to the kitchen, moving quietly so as not to awaken the others in the house.

This was the only time of day when the kitchen was quiet and cool. As the day progressed, heat was produced by the cookstove. Heat seeped in from outside through the screened door and the window above the sink. Even Ella's own energy acted as a generator.

Proportionately with the thermometer, the noise level rose, so that by suppertime, the kitchen, which was the heart of the house, took on a pulsating life of its own and didn't settle into cool repose until Ella extinguished the overhead light for the final time, most often hours after her boarders had retired.

This morning, she didn't pause to enjoy either the relative coolness or the silence. Having put on her apron, she lit the oven, put the coffee on to brew, then mixed the biscuit dough. Margaret arrived right on time, and after removing her hat and hanging it on the peg inside the door, and gratefully taking a tin cup of sweetened coffee from Ella, she went back outside to fill the washing machine with water for the first load of laundry.

The prospect of buying an electric-powered washing machine was so remote that Ella didn't even dream about it. For her foreseeable future she must continue using the one with the hand-crank wringer that had been her mother's. Suds and rinse water from the tub were drained into a ditch that ran alongside the shed where the washer was housed.

On a summer day like today, the washing shed became stifling by midmorning. But wet laundry seemed heavier when one's hands were raw and numb from cold during the winter months. In any season, laundry days were dreaded. By nightfall her back would be aching.

Solly, still in his pajamas, wandered into the kitchen while she was frying bacon.

Breakfast was served at eight.

By nine o'clock everyone had been fed, the dishes washed, dried, and put away. Ella set a pot of mustard greens on the stove to simmer all day, cooked a pan of Faultless starch, then, taking Solly with her, went outside to hang up the first basket of laundry that Margaret had washed, rinsed, and wrung out.

It was almost eleven o'clock when she went inside to check on things in the kitchen. While she was adding a little more salt to the greens, someone pulled the bell at her front door. As she walked along the dim center hall, she dried her hands on her apron and glanced at herself in the wall mirror. Her face was flushed and damp from the heat, and her heavy bun had defied the pins and slipped down onto her nape, but she continued to the door without stopping to primp.

On the other side of the threshold, squinting at her through the screened door, was Dr. Kincaid. "Morning, Mrs. Barron." His white straw hat had a natty red cloth band, striated with generations of sweat stains. He removed it and held it against his chest in a rather courtly manner.

She was surprised to see the doctor on her porch, but still nothing signaled her that this would be an extraordinary day.

Dr. Kincaid's office was in the center of town on Hill Street, but he also made house calls, usually to deliver a baby, sometimes to keep a contagious patient from spreading his infection through Gilead, their town of two thousand.

Ella herself had summoned the doctor to the house a couple of years ago when one of her boarders fell out of his bed during the middle of the night. Mr. Blackwell, an elderly gentleman who fortunately had been more embarrassed than injured, protested even as Dr. Kincaid agreed with Ella that he probably should be thoroughly examined just as a precaution. Mr. Blackwell no longer lived with her. Shortly after that incident, his family had moved him to a home for the elderly in Waco. Mr. Blackwell had futilely protested his involuntary relocation, too.

Had one of her boarders sent for the doctor today? Little in the house escaped Ella's notice, but she'd been outside most of the morning, so it was possible that one of the sisters had used the telephone without her knowledge.

"Good morning, Dr. Kincaid. Did one of the Dunnes send for you?"

"No. I'm not here on a sick call."

"Then what can I do for you?"

"Is this a bad time?"

She thought of the clothes piled into baskets and ready to be starched, but the starch needed a while longer to cool. "Not at all. Come in." She reached up to unlatch the screened door and pushed it open.

Dr. Kincaid turned to his right and made a come-forward motion with his hat. Ella was unaware of the other man's presence until he stepped around the large fern at the side of the front door and into her range of vision.

Her first impression of him was how tall and lean he was. One could almost say he looked underfed. He was dressed in a black suit with a white shirt and black necktie, and was holding a black felt fedora. She thought his clothes looked severe and out of season for such a hot morning, especially compared to Dr. Kincaid's seersucker suit and white hat with the red band.

The doctor made the introduction. "Mrs. Barron, this is Mr. Rainwater."

He inclined his head. "Ma'am."

"Mr. Rainwater."

She moved aside and indicated for them to come inside. Dr. Kincaid allowed the other man to go in ahead of him. A few steps into the foyer, he stopped to let his eyes adjust to the relative darkness. Then he took in his surroundings as he idly threaded the brim of his hat through long, slender fingers.

"In here, please." Ella stepped around her two guests and motioned them into the formal parlor. "Have a seat."

"We thought we heard the doorbell."

The chirping voice brought Ella around. The Misses Dunne, Violet and Pearl, were standing on the bottom stair. In their pastel print dresses and old-fashioned shoes, they were virtually interchangeable. Each had a nimbus of white hair. Their veined, spotted hands clutched matching handkerchiefs, daintily hemmed and hand-embroidered by their mother, they'd told Ella.

With unabashed curiosity, the two were looking beyond Ella to catch a glimpse of the visitors. Having callers was an event.

"Is that Dr. Kincaid?" asked Pearl, the more inquisitive of the two. "Hello, Dr. Kincaid," she called.

"Good morning, Miss Pearl."

"Who's that with you?"

Miss Violet frowned at her sister with reproof. "We were coming down to play gin rummy until lunch," she whispered to Ella. "Will we disturb?"

"Not at all."

Ella asked them to use the informal parlor and led them to it. When they were situated at the card table, she said, "Please excuse us, ladies," and pulled together the heavy oak pocket doors that divided the large room in half. She rejoined the two men in the formal side, which overlooked the front porch. Despite her invitation for them to sit down, they had remained standing.

Dr. Kincaid was fanning himself with his hat. Ella switched on the fan on the table in the corner, directed the stream of air toward him, then motioned the men toward a pair of wingback chairs. "Please."

They sat when she did.

This being summer, and wash day, she hadn't put on stockings that morning. Embarrassed by her bare legs, she crossed her ankles and pulled her feet beneath the chair. "Would you like some lemonade? Or tea?"

"That sounds awfully good, Mrs. Barron, but I'm afraid I have to pass," the doctor said. "I've got patients to see at the clinic."

She looked at Mr. Rainwater.

"No thank you," he said.

Returning to the kitchen would have given her an opportunity to remove her apron, which had a damp patch where she'd dried her hands, and to pin her bun more securely. But since her guests had declined the offer of a drink, she was stuck looking untidy for the remainder of their visit, the purpose of which hadn't yet been stated. She wondered what Solly was up to and how long this unexpected meeting was going to take. She hoped Mr. Rainwater wasn't a salesman. She didn't have time to sit through his pitch, only to say no to whatever it was he was peddling.

The smell of simmering mustard greens was strong, even here in the front parlor. The doctor withdrew a large white handkerchief from his coat pocket and used it to blot sweat from his balding head. A yellow jacket flew into the window screen and continued angrily to try to go through it. The hum of the electric fan seemed as loud as a buzz saw.

She was relieved when Dr. Kincaid cleared his throat and said, "I heard you lost a boarder."

"That's right. Mrs. Morton went to live with an ailing sister. Somewhere in eastern Louisiana, I believe."

"Quite a piece from here," he remarked.

"Her nephew came to escort her on the train."

"Nice for her, I'm sure. Have you had anyone speak for her room?"

"She only left the day before yesterday. I haven't had time to advertise."

"Well then, that's good, that's good," the doctor said and began fanning himself enthusiastically, as though in celebration of something.

Discerning now the purpose for their call, she looked at Mr. Rainwater. He sat leaning slightly forward with both feet on the floor. His black shoes were shined, she noticed. His thick, dark hair was smoothed back off his face, but one strand, as straight and shiny as a satin ribbon, had defiantly flopped over his broad forehead. His cheekbones were pronounced, his eyebrows as sleek and black as crows' wings. He had startling blue eyes, and they were steady on her.

"Are you interested in lodging, Mr. Rainwater?"

"Yes. I need a place to stay."

"I haven't had a chance to give the vacant room a thorough cleaning, but as soon as it's ready, I'd be happy to show it to you."

"I'm not particular." He smiled, showing teeth that were very white, although slightly crooked on the top. "I'll take the room as is."

"Oh, I'm afraid I couldn't let you have it now," she said quickly. "Not until I've aired the bedding, scrubbed everything, polished the floor. I have very high standards."

"For boarders or cleanliness?"

"For both."

"Which is why I've brought him to you," the doctor said hastily. "I told Mr. Rainwater that you keep an immaculate house and run a tight ship. To say nothing of the excellent meals your boarders enjoy. He desires a place that's well maintained. A peaceful and quiet house."

Just then, from the direction of the kitchen, came a terrible racket followed by a bloodcurdling scream.

TWO

Ella was out of her chair like a shot. "Excuse me."

She ran from the parlor and down the hallway, bursting into the kitchen, where Solly was standing in the middle of the floor, screeching at the top of his voice and holding his left arm away from his body as stiff as a ramrod.

Hot starch had spattered his arm from wrist to shoulder. Some had splashed onto his chest, plastering his cotton shirt to his skin. The pan which had been on the stove was now lying overturned on the floor. The sticky blue stuff was oozing out of it, forming a wide puddle.

Heedless of the mess, Ella lifted her son and hugged him to her. "Oh no, oh, God. Solly, Solly, oh, sweetheart. Oh, Lord."

"Cold water." Dr. Kincaid had rushed into the kitchen practically on her heels and had immediately assessed the situation. He pushed her toward the sink and turned on the cold water spout, forcing Solly's arm beneath the stream.

"Do you have ice?"

Mr. Rainwater addressed the question to Margaret, who'd come rushing in from the backyard, calling on Jesus for help even before determining the nature of the catastrophe.

Since Margaret seemed incapable of answering him, Ella shouted above Solly's screams. "There's ice in the box. A whole block delivered just this morning."

She and Dr. Kincaid continued to struggle with the boy to keep his burned arm under the gush of cold water. Ella splashed handfuls of it onto his shirt, trying to neutralize the starch that was burning him through the thin fabric.

None of this was easily done. They had to battle Solly, whose right arm was flailing about, often connecting painfully with either Ella or the doctor. The boy was also trying to butt heads with them and kicking his feet. Several pieces of crockery and china were knocked off the drainboard and onto the floor, breaking in the widening puddle of starch.

"This will help." Mr. Rainwater moved up beside Ella with a chunk of freshly chipped ice. While she and Dr. Kincaid held Solly's arm as still as possible, Mr. Rainwater rubbed the ice up and down her child's arm, which now bore ugly red splotches.

The ice cooled the burns, and eventually Solly stopped screaming, but he continued to bob his head rhythmically. The doctor turned off the tap. Ella noticed that the sleeves of his coat were wet to his elbows and realized that her apron and dress were drenched as well.

"Thank you." She took what was left of the chunk of ice from Mr. Rainwater and continued to rub it up and down Solly's arm as she carried him to a chair and sat down with him on her lap. She hugged him close and kissed the top of his head as she cradled him tightly against her chest. Even then it took several minutes before he stopped the rhythmic bobbing of his head.

From the open doorway, the two Dunne spinsters cooed commiseration and encouragement.

Margaret was holding the hem of her apron to her lips with one hand, the other pink palm was raised beseechingly toward the ceiling. She was crying loudly and praying plaintively, "Jesus, he'p this poor baby. Lord Jesus, he'p this child."

Ella was grateful for Margaret's prayers and hoped the Lord was listening, but the loud praying was adding to the confusion. "Margaret, please bring me one of his candy sticks," she said.

Her quiet tone cut through Margaret's fervent litany. She ceased praying, smoothed her apron back into place, and went into the pantry, where Ella kept a jar of candy sticks hidden behind canisters of flour and sugar. If Solly spotted the candy, he demanded it by lying on the floor and kicking until he either exhausted himself or exhausted Ella to the point of giving in just to restore the peace.

The candy sticks were reserved for times of crisis. Like now.

Margaret was choking back sobs. "It's my fault. He was playin' there in the dirt. You know how he likes to dig with that big wood spoon? I turned my back, couldn't've been more'n half a minute, to throw that bedsheet over the clothesline. Next I know, he's in the house a-screamin'. I'm sorry, Miss Ella. I—"

"It wasn't your fault, Margaret. I know how quickly he can disappear."

Margaret muttered on about how she was to blame as she brought the candy jar from the pantry, lifted off the metal lid, and extended it to Solly. "Margaret ain't ever gonna forgive herself for this. No she ain't. What flavor you want, baby doll?"

Solly remained unaware of Margaret, so Ella selected for him, a white stick with orange stripes. She didn't hand it to him directly but laid it on the table. He picked it up and began to lick. Everyone in the kitchen sighed with relief.

"Let me take a look at the burns."

"No." Ella held up her hand to prevent the doctor from moving any closer and setting Solly off again. "The spots aren't blistering, and the starch had been cooling for over two hours. It wasn't that hot. When he pulled the pan off the stove and the starch splashed on him, I think it frightened him more than anything."

"It's a good thing it wasn't—"

Miss Pearl's comment was stopped abruptly, probably when she got an elbow in the ribs from her more tactful sister. But Ella knew what Miss Pearl was thinking, what everyone including herself was thinking: It was a good thing Solly hadn't pulled the stewing greens off the stove and onto himself.

Ella smoothed her hand over her son's head, but he dodged the caress. The rejection pierced her heart, but she looked at the others and smiled bravely. "I think the crisis has passed."

"I have some salve at the clinic," the doctor said. "Even though the skin's not blistered, it wouldn't hurt to keep it lubricated for a day or two."

Ella nodded and looked over at Mr. Rainwater, who was hovering near the stove, as though guarding against another accident. "The ice helped. Thank you."

He nodded.

She said, "About the room—"

"See, I told you he was to be a new boarder." Miss Pearl spoke to her sister in a whisper which everyone heard.

"We'll excuse ourselves until lunch." Miss Violet grasped

her sister's arm with enough pressure to make her wince and practically dragged her toward the staircase. Miss Pearl was still whispering excitedly as they made their way up. "He seems awfully nice, don't you think, Sister? Very clean fingernails. I wonder who his people are."

Ella eased Solly off her lap and into the chair in which she was seated. She made a futile attempt to smooth back strands of hair that had shaken loose from her bun. Responding to the humidity created by the cooking pot of greens, her hair had formed unruly spirals on both sides of her face.

"As I was saying, Mr. Rainwater, I haven't had time to give the room a thorough cleaning. If you're wanting to move in immediately—"

"I am."

"You can't."

"Then when?"

"When the room meets my standards."

The statement seemed to amuse him, and she wondered if his quick grin was mocking her standards or her pride in them.

In either case, she resented it. "In light of what the last quarter hour has been like, I'm surprised you're still interested in securing a room in my house, especially if it's peace and quiet you're after. You haven't even seen the room yet."

"Then let's take a look," Dr. Kincaid said. "But I really must get back to the clinic soon."

Mr. Rainwater said, "You don't have to stay, Murdy."

Dr. Kincaid's first name was Murdock, but Ella had never heard him addressed as Murdy, not even by close acquaintances.

"No, no, I want to help any way I can." The doctor turned to her. "Mrs. Barron?"

She glanced down at Solly, who had eaten half his candy stick. Margaret, sensing her hesitation, said, "You go on with the gentlemen. I'll keep an eagle eye on this boy. I swear I won't take my eyes off him."

Reluctantly Ella led the two men from the kitchen and up the stairs, then down the hallway to the room at the end of it. Opening the door, she said, "It's got a nice southern exposure. You can catch the breeze."

The sheer curtains now catching the breeze were ruffled. The wallpaper had a yellow cabbage rose pattern, and the iron bed looked too short for Mr. Rainwater. In fact, even though he was slender, the room looked smaller with him standing in its center, much smaller than when Mrs. Morton had occupied it.

But he seemed either not to notice or not to care about the feminine decor or the limited size of the bed, the room, or the narrow closet. He looked out the window, nodded, then turned back to her and the doctor. "This will do."

"You would share a bathroom with Mr. Hastings."

"Chester Hastings," Dr. Kincaid supplied. "Extremely nice man. He's not in town much. Notions salesman. Travels all over."

"I don't have a problem with sharing a bathroom," Mr. Rainwater said.

On the way downstairs, Ella told him the cost for room and board, and by the time they reached the ground floor he had agreed to it.

"Splendid," Dr. Kincaid said. "I'll let the two of you work out the particulars about moving in and so forth."

Ella hesitated and glanced toward the kitchen. Margaret was softly humming a hymn, which usually soothed Solly. Comforting him would also help alleviate Margaret's guilt, so Ella decided she could spare another few minutes.

"I'll see you out." She led the way to the front door, but when she got there, she discovered that only Dr. Kincaid had followed her. Behind them the hallway was empty. Presumably Mr. Rainwater had ducked into the parlor, waiting there to discuss the details of his occupancy.

"Can I have a word, Mrs. Barron?" the doctor asked. Only moments ago, he had seemed in such a hurry to leave that she looked at him curiously as he pushed open the screened door and ushered her out onto the porch.

The overhang formed by the second story of the house had trapped the heat as well as the heady fragrance of gardenia. The shrub, laden with creamy white blossoms, grew in a pot she kept at the end of the porch.

Two summers ago she'd had a boarder who complained of the fragrance being cloying and giving him headaches. Ella attributed his headaches less to the aromatic blossoms and more to the corn liquor he sipped from a silver flask when he thought no one was looking. When she reminded him that she didn't allow spirits in the house, he'd been affronted.

"Are you referring to my cough remedy, Mrs. Barron?"

Short of calling him a liar, she couldn't challenge him further, but he also never again complained about the gardenias. She'd been relieved when he'd moved out and the more genial Mr. Hastings had moved in.

Again the doctor dabbed his bald head with his handkerchief. "I wanted to speak to you in private."

"About Solly?"

"Well, that, yes."

They'd had this discussion many times before. Bracing for

an argument, she clasped her hands at her waist. "I refuse to place him in an institution, Dr. Kincaid."

"I haven't suggested—"

"I also refuse to keep him medicated."

"So you've told me. Many times."

"Then please stop trying to persuade me otherwise."

"What happened just now—"

"Could have happened to any child," she said. "Remember when the Hinnegar boy turned that kerosene lamp over on himself last winter?"

"That boy is two years old, Mrs. Barron. Solly is ten."

"His birthday is still months away."

"Close enough." Softening his tone, the doctor continued. "I'm well aware of the perils inherent to childhood. Based on what I've seen during my years of general practice, it's amazing to me that any of us reaches adulthood."

He paused, took a breath, then looked at her kindly. "But your boy is particularly susceptible to mishaps. Even at his age, Solly can't understand the dangers associated with something like pulling a pan of hot starch off the stove. And then when there is an accident, his reaction is a violent outburst. As it was today."

"He was burned, he was screaming in pain. Anyone would scream."

"By my speaking to you plainly, please don't think I'm being insensitive or unnecessarily cruel. It's your situation that's cruel. The fact is, without medication to suppress your son's . . . impulses, he could harm himself and others, especially when he's in the throes of one of his fits."

"I keep careful watch over him to prevent that."

"I don't question how dutiful—"

"It's not my duty, it's my privilege. Only the running of

this house prevents me from devoting every waking moment to Solly. This morning was an exception, not the rule. I was unexpectedly called away."

That was a subtle reminder that he was responsible for her distraction, but the doctor ignored the rebuke.

"You bring me to the next point, Mrs. Barron. This constant vigilance is also detrimental to *your* health. How long can you keep it up?"

"For as long as Solly needs supervision."

"Which in all likelihood will be for the rest of his life. What happens when he outgrows you and you can no longer physically restrain him?"

She forced herself to unclench her hands. In a slow and deliberate voice she said, "The medications you're suggesting to suppress his impulses would also inhibit his ability to learn."

Her saying that caused the doctor's eyes to become even kinder, sadder, more pitying.

She took umbrage. "I know you doubt Solly's capacity to learn, Dr. Kincaid. I do not. I won't rob him of the opportunity just because it would make my life easier. I won't have him drugged into a stupor, where he would be breathing but little else. What kind of life would he have?"

"What kind of life do *you* have?" he asked gently.

She drew herself up to her full height. Her face was hot with indignation. "I appreciate your professional opinion, Dr. Kincaid. But that's all it is, an *opinion*. No one really knows what Solly is or isn't capable of understanding and retaining. But as his mother, I have a better perception of his abilities than anyone. So I must do what I think is best for him."

Yielding the battle if not the war, the doctor glanced away from her toward the clump of larkspur growing at the edge of her yard. Their blue spikes were wilting in the noon heat. "Send Margaret 'round for that salve," he finally said.

"Thank you."

"No charge."

"Thank you."

The street was deserted except for a spotted brown and white dog that was trotting alongside a wagon driven by an elderly black man and pulled by a pair of plodding mules. The man tipped his hat to them as the wagon rolled past. They waved back at him. Ella didn't know him, but the doctor addressed him by name and called out a greeting.

"If that's all, Dr. Kincaid, I need to set out lunch."

He turned back to her. "Actually, there is something else, Mrs. Barron. About Mr. Rainwater."

Other than his name, and his willingness to pay her fee for room and board, she knew nothing about the man. She was taking him in as a boarder based solely upon Dr. Kincaid's implied recommendation. "Is he a man of good character?"

"Impeccable character."

"You've known him for a long time?"

"He's my wife's late cousin's boy. I guess that makes him some sort of a second or third cousin by marriage."

"I guessed he might be an old friend or family member. He called you Murdy."

Absently he nodded. "Family nickname."

"Is he in the medical profession, too?"

"No. He was a cotton broker."

"*Was?*" Was Mr. Rainwater a victim of the Depression, one of the thousands of men in the nation who were out of work? "If he's unemployed, how does he plan to pay his rent? I can't afford—"

"He's not without funds. He's . . ." The doctor looked toward the retreating wagon and continued watching it as it rounded the corner. Coming back to her, he said, "The fact is, he won't be needing the room in your house for long."

She stared at him, waiting.

Softly he said, "He's dying."

THREE

"Please, Mr. Rainwater. Leave that."

He was crouched, picking pieces of broken china off the kitchen linoleum. He glanced up at her but continued what he was doing. "I'm afraid the boy will hurt himself again."

"Margaret and I will tend to the mess, and to Solly."

Margaret was at the stove drizzling bacon grease from that morning's breakfast into the greens. Solly was sitting in his customary chair at the kitchen table, rocking back and forth, fiddling with a yo-yo that Margaret must have given him from his box of toys. He wound the string around his index finger, unwound it. His concentration was fixed on the winding and rewinding.

The crisis had passed, and he didn't appear to be suffering any lasting effects, but would she know if he were? She had to take his passivity as a good sign. Looking at his blond head bowed over the yo-yo, she felt the familiar pinching sensation

26

deep within her heart, a mix of unqualified love and the fear that even that might not be sufficient to protect him.

Mr. Rainwater came to his feet and held out his hands. Ella took the dustpan off the nail from which it hung on the wall and extended it to him. He carefully placed the chips of broken dishware in it. "Those are the larger pieces. There are some slivers I couldn't pick out of the starch."

"We'll watch for them when we clean up."

He turned to the sink and washed the starch off his hands, then dried them on a dish towel. She would have felt awkward making herself so at home in someone else's kitchen, especially a stranger's. He seemed to suffer no such self-consciousness.

She set the dustpan on the floor in the corner. "Margaret, could you get out the lunch things while I speak with Mr. Rainwater?"

"Yes, ma'am. You want me to get this baby's lunch, too?"

"Please. Peel an orange and section it. A butter and grape jelly sandwich, cut in half. Put them on the blue plate he likes."

"Yes, ma'am. You tend to the gentleman here." She smiled at Mr. Rainwater, obviously pleased that he was about to join the household. His willingness to help during an emergency situation had earned her hard-won approval. "Them sheets need hanging, but they can keep till after lunch."

"Thank you, Margaret." Ella turned and gestured the man toward the hallway. "Mr. Rainwater?"

"We can talk here."

Ella preferred not to discuss business in the kitchen, where, as anticipated, the temperature had climbed. She was also worried about the sheets in the washtub that needed to be wrung through the wringer, probably twice, before being hung on the clothesline to dry. She was afraid that Margaret would get heavy-handed with the bacon grease, which she was prone to do. Margaret was also a gossip. On several occasions Ella had been forced to chide her for sharing personal information about their boarders and about Ella herself.

Her major concern, however, was Solly, although the red marks on his skin had faded so they were barely visible now, and the burns didn't seem to be hurting him. For the moment he was pacified.

She wasn't. The accident with the starch had left her frazzled and distracted. She'd been further shaken by what Dr. Kincaid had told her about Mr. Rainwater. Although her livelihood depended on keeping her house filled to capacity, to take in a dying man was an unappealing prospect on numerous levels, not the least of which was that she already had her hands full, what with keeping her other boarders happy and dealing with Solly.

However, Mr. Rainwater's unfortunate circumstance was the only hindrance to his being a suitable boarder. On that basis alone, how could she live with her conscience if she refused to rent the room to him?

Dr. Kincaid should have informed her of his condition first, before she'd agreed to let him the room. Mr. Rainwater should have told her himself. The omission had left her at a distinct disadvantage, and he was placing her at one now by discussing business in the presence of her talkative maid.

Trying to keep the resentment from her voice, she said, "You'll find envelopes in your nightstand drawer. There's a collection box for your rent on a table under the stairs. I collect the rent each Monday, but you'll pay me the first week in advance before you move in. Is that satisfactory?"

"Yes. Fine."

"To avoid confusion, don't forget to write your name on the envelope before leaving it in the box."

"I won't."

Knowing what she now did, she found his steady gaze even more unsettling. She was relieved when Margaret drew his attention. "Here, sweet pea. Here's your lunch fixed just the way you like it." She set the blue plate on the table in front of Solly.

Solly didn't respond either to Margaret or to the food. He continued to rock, continued to wind the yo-yo string around his finger.

"About meals," Ella said, drawing Mr. Rainwater's attention back to her. "A full breakfast is served each morning at eight o'clock, but you can get coffee here in the kitchen before that. Dinner is at six-thirty. So as not to waste food, I would appreciate being notified if you plan to have a meal out."

"I doubt I'll have any meals out."

If he hadn't been there, she would have pulled the pins from her bun and shaken it loose. It had slipped farther down onto her neck, where it felt hot and heavy. "For lunch, I put out cold cuts, cheese, fruit. Sometimes leftovers." She motioned toward Margaret, who was unwrapping slices of ham from waxed butcher paper. "It's on the dining table between noon and one, and it's first come, first served." She glanced at the wall clock. "I'm running a bit late today, but the Dunnes rarely eat more than a piece of fruit anyway, and Mr. Hastings is out of town."

"Are they your only boarders, besides myself?"

She nodded. "The sisters share the largest room, at the opposite end of the hall from yours. Mr. Hastings has the room at the top of the stairs."

"And you and Solly?"

"Here on the ground floor. On Sunday," she said briskly, "I serve the main meal at two o'clock. That gives me time to return from church. Everyone is on their own for Sunday night supper, but the kitchen is open for your use. I only ask that you clean up after yourself."

"Of course."

"Is there anything you shouldn't eat?" She asked that of all her new boarders, although it might appear to him that she had singled him out because of his illness.

As though following her thoughts, he gave a faint smile. "I can eat anything, and I'm not a picky eater."

"Any questions so far?"

"When may I move in?"

Dodging that for the moment, she pressed on. "Bed linens are changed once a week. I ask that you use only three towels between wash days. Keep the bathroom tidy as a courtesy to Mr. Hastings. He's expected to do the same for you. If you have any complaints, bring them to me.

"I don't allow liquor in the house. I expect basic, common courtesy and sensitivity to the other tenants' privacy and comfort. If you have visitors, you can receive them in the formal parlor, but please give me notice. Arrangements can be made for refreshments to be served to guests. For a nominal charge you can have a guest for dinner, but only if I'm informed ahead of time."

"I won't have any visitors, no guests for dinner."

His eyes burned as intensely, as blue, as the pilot light on her stove. They arrested her for a moment, then she looked away. "I'll give you the post office box number so you can pass it along to your family and friends."

"I'll be very surprised if I receive any mail."

"Well, in case you do, only I have the key to the box. I'll leave your mail in your room. You can rely on my discretion."

"I'm certain of that."

"Does all of this sound acceptable, Mr. Rainwater?"

Having waited patiently for her to go over the rules of the house, he repeated, "When may I move in?"

That was the third time he'd asked. Understandably. Time would be an issue to a man for whom, according to Dr. Kincaid, time was short.

"Tuesday."

"This is Thursday."

"As I explained, the room needs to be cleaned. Can you continue to stay with Dr. and Mrs. Kincaid until the room is ready?"

"I've been with them for two nights already. They've been very hospitable and have given me the use of their boys' bedroom. But the boys are having to sleep on pallets in the living room, inconveniencing everyone. I'd like to move in tomorrow at the latest."

"The room won't be ready by then. This is wash day. Margaret and I can't postpone doing the laundry in order to prepare the room for you. The furniture must be removed so the floor can be scrubbed. The mattress and pillows need to be taken out and aired." With irritation, she brushed back a lock of hair that was clinging to her cheek. "I can't possibly get everything done by tomorrow."

"My new preacher's looking for work."

Ella looked toward Margaret. "What?"

"Brother Calvin," she said. "He just come to town to take over the pulpit. But our congregation can't pay him nothing. He's sleeping on a member's porch, and they's feeding him, but he's wanting to earn some money so he can get a place of his own and move his wife here. She's down in South Texas with her folks, and he's missing her something awful. For a little bit of nothing he'd do them chores for you, Miz Barron. You ought not to be doing all that heavy lifting anyhow, and my back's hurting just thinking about hauling that mattress down them stairs and back up again. Why'n't you let me fetch Brother Calvin?"

Ella glanced at Mr. Rainwater, who was following this conversation with interest. He said, "I'd be willing to pay Brother Calvin's fee."

Margaret smiled as though the matter had been settled. She headed toward the hallway, where the telephone was. "I'll call over to the store right now." To Mr. Rainwater she said, "Randall's Dry Goods and Grocery is where my boy, Jimmy, works. While he's on a delivery, he can run right over to where the preacher's stayin' and tell him to get hisself over here."

When Margaret was out of earshot, Mr. Rainwater said to Ella, "I hope that's all right with you."

It wasn't. This was her house. All decisions regarding it were hers to make. But it seemed that nothing was normal this morning. Everything was out of whack. She was being swept along by an unusual series of events. In fact she felt overtaken by them, and that sense of floundering alarmed her. Routine wasn't just a preference, it was a necessity.

But in the grand scheme of things, retaining the services of Brother Calvin was a small matter, and she would look peevish to object to so workable a plan, especially since Mr. Rainwater had offered to pay for the man's services.

However, she wasn't quite ready to concede. "I would prefer to do the work myself, Mr. Rainwater."

"Because your standards are so high."

"I'm not afraid of hard work."

"No one would doubt that."

"But since time is a factor . . ."

She hadn't intended to mention his limited time. She let the sentence dwindle without finishing it. Embarrassment made her face feel even hotter than it already did.

He said, "This is a good plan. It will save you a lot of labor. It will spare Margaret's back. And it will hasten Brother Calvin's reunion with his wife."

Again, she noticed the gleam of amusement in his eyes, and she thought that, if she smiled, he would also. But she didn't, so neither did he. "And it accommodates you," she pointed out.

"It does, yes."

She sighed defeat. "All right. But if you would give me through tomorrow morning, I would appreciate it."

"How about four o'clock tomorrow afternoon?"

"Four? Yes, good. By then I'll have the room ready."

"I'll be sure to come with cash in hand. To cover Brother Calvin's charges and the first week's rent."

He grinned, but she didn't return it. Instead, she motioned him toward the hall, indicating that their business was concluded.

"I can go out the back way."

Nodding, she walked him to the screened back door. As he went down the steps, he put on his hat. At the bottom of the steps, he turned back and doffed the brim. "Mrs. Barron."

"Mr. Rainwater. I hope you'll be comfortable here."

She had other duties to attend to, the first of which was to see that Solly ate his lunch. But for some reason, she didn't turn away. She maintained eye contact with the man who would share her address for the last weeks of his life. Did her pity show? she wondered. It must have.

He said, "He told you, didn't he? Murdy told you about me."

Being coy wasn't in Ella's nature. Besides, she wouldn't insult the man by lying. "He thought I should know."

He nodded, not only in confirmation of what he suspected but also in what seemed to be approval of her straightforwardness. "I'd thank you not to tell the others. Knowing makes people uncomfortable, they start watching what they say. In any case, I don't want a fuss made over it. I don't want to be treated differently from anyone else."

"I won't say anything to anyone."

"Thank you."

"There's no need to thank me, Mr. Rainwater."

"See what I mean?" he said, grinning. "You're already making concessions for me."

She had the grace to look abashed.

His grin held for several moments, then he turned serious again. "Does he talk?"

"What?"

"Your son."

He motioned with his head. She turned. Behind her, Solly was still at the table. His lunch remained untouched. He was winding the yo-yo string around his finger, unwinding it, winding it again as he rocked forward and back to a beat that only he could hear.

She came around to Mr. Rainwater again and shook her head. "No. He doesn't talk."

"Well," he said pleasantly, "I find that most people who do often have nothing worthwhile to say."

His easy dismissal of Solly's limitations was almost more difficult to withstand than the rude, curious stares of strangers, and she reacted with a totally unexpected rush of tears. Perhaps he saw them and wanted to spare her embarrassment, because he said no more, only touched the brim of his hat again, turned, and walked away.

FOUR

Brother Calvin Taylor turned out to be a godsend, and not just to the AME church.

The preacher was a tall and robust man in his late twenties, with an engaging manner and a wide smile, made even more brilliant by a gold front tooth. Ella wondered if members of his congregation were distracted by his tooth while he was preaching, if it would be like a swinging pocket watch with a hypnotic effect.

But once she heard his speaking voice, she decided that little could distract his flock from his divinely inspired words. It was the voice of a prophet, the bass tones rolling like thunder off a hillside. She imagined it reverberating inside the church house, waking the dozing, frightening sinners into repentance, and filling the faithful with renewed devotion.

He had indeed made a favorable impact on the congregation. When Margaret formally introduced Brother Calvin to Ella, she boasted that the church's attendance had increased threefold since he'd taken over the pulpit.

"Any given Sunday, there ain't an empty pew."

The young preacher reacted to her praise with appropriate humility, crediting God with his success. "The Lord is blessing us in tremendous ways."

Ella liked him immediately, and put him straight to work, even though the Dunne sisters might very well swoon when they saw a colored man inside the house. Ella didn't share their prejudices. She recalled the occasion when she first realized that the privileges accorded the races were terribly inequitable.

Her father had taken her to the picture show in Waco, and she'd wanted to sit in the balcony. He'd explained that the balcony was restricted to colored people. She'd protested, saying that wasn't fair. She was objecting to the injustice to herself for not being allowed to sit where she chose. But her father, misinterpreting, placed his arm across her shoulders and smiled down at her. "No, it isn't, Ella. Not fair at all. And I'm proud you feel that way."

She hadn't been taught to have prejudices, so she didn't. But as she got older, she came to understand that her viewpoint on racial matters wasn't shared by most.

The preacher soon proved he wasn't all talk. By the end of the day he had scrubbed and polished the floor of the vacant room. "May as well do the hallway, while I'm at it," he'd said. It, too, was hand-buffed to a shine.

At suppertime, Ella gave him a plate of food to eat in the kitchen while she served the Dunne sisters in the dining room. She noticed that the pastor said grace over the food before he ate. When he finished his meal, he carried the bedding in from the backyard, where it had been airing all afternoon, and replaced it in the room that was to become Mr. Rainwater's.

Before Brother Calvin left, he told her he would be back early in the morning to help Margaret with any other chores that needed to be done before the new boarder moved in. "By four o'clock, that room will be sparkling. I promise."

He kept his promise. All the work was done to Ella's satisfaction. However, she made up the bed herself. Not only was she particular about how a bed was made but she derived pleasure from the fresh-air-and-sunshine smell of the sheets and pillowcases.

Mr. Rainwater arrived at the appointed time. The Dunnes had gone to the lending library, which was a converted panel truck that came to Gilead only one afternoon every two weeks. Margaret was ironing in the kitchen while keeping an eye on Solly. Mr. Hastings was still out of town.

Except for the grandfather clock in the formal parlor softly chiming the hour of four o'clock, the house was hushed when Ella unlatched the front screened door for him. They exchanged pleasantries, then she led him upstairs. Their footfalls echoed hollowly on the newly polished floor of the hall.

He paused in the open doorway of the bedroom and looked it over. He took in every detail, including the sprig of honeysuckle that Margaret had left in a vase of water on the bureau. Then he turned to Ella. "You were right to hold to your standards, Mrs. Barron. The room is much nicer now. Thank you."

"You're welcome."

"I realize I asked a lot of you to make it ready, but I wanted to move in sooner rather than later."

She merely nodded, afraid that if she said something

in reference to the time frame, it would come out sounding wrong.

He passed her a white envelope with his name printed on it in black ink. "The first week's rent. Let me know what I owe Brother Calvin."

Then he carried two canvas suitcases into the room and gently closed the door.

"Northeast Texas. About halfway between Dallas and Texarkana."

Throughout the evening meal, the Dunnes had peppered Mr. Rainwater with questions. Ella was stacking their empty dinner plates on a tray when Miss Violet inquired where he was from.

Miss Pearl, who had been gazing dreamily across the table at him, said, "That's good cotton-growing country up there."

"He knows that, Sister," Violet said. "He's a cotton broker, after all."

"I realize that," Pearl returned with asperity. "I'm just remarking."

To prevent a sibling quarrel, Ella tactfully intervened. "Should I bring out cream with the berry cobbler, Miss Pearl?"

"Oh, cream, yes, please. Don't you think cobbler is best served with cream, Mr. Rainwater?"

"I certainly do." He glanced up at Ella, the corners of his lips twitching to contain a smile. "Cream for me, too, please."

"Coffee?"

"Please."

She hefted the tray.

Mr. Rainwater stood up. "Can I help you with that?"

"No."

The word came out much more emphatically than Ella had intended, and everyone in the room, even Ella herself, was taken aback by her tone. The sisters were gaping not only at her but also at the new boarder. Apparently they were as surprised as Ella by his unprecedented offer to help.

To hide her embarrassment, she ducked her head and murmured, "No, thank you, Mr. Rainwater," then hastily headed for the kitchen.

As she left the room, she overheard Miss Violet delicately clear her throat before inquiring, "What about your family, Mr. Rainwater?"

"My mother and father are both deceased, and I'm an only child."

"Oh, that's unfortunate," Pearl said. "Violet and I have only each other. The rest of our family has died out."

The kitchen door swung shut, preventing Ella from hearing Mr. Rainwater's comment on that.

"Them ol' ladies is goin' drive that man plumb crazy with all them questions about hisself," Margaret said, shaking her head.

"I heard you asking him some questions earlier."

"I's just being polite," she grumbled. When she glanced across at Ella, she did a double take. "You all right?"

"All right? Of course. Why?"

"Your cheeks look hot. I hope you ain't coming down with that bad summer fever. It's keeping some folks prostrate for weeks."

"I don't have a fever. Have you spooned up the cobbler yet?"

"Ain't I always got dessert ready before I start washing up?" The maid used her shoulder to point out the dishes of cobbler on the counter, waiting to be placed on a serving tray. "What about them shutters on the front windows?"

"What about them?"

"I tol' you. Brother Calvin offered to paint them."

Ella added the coffee service to the tray. "I can't afford to have them painted right now."

"They look shabby."

"I know they *need* painting, Margaret, but—"

"Brother Calvin said he'd do it for cheap. It was nice of him to bring us those dewberries. Picked 'em hisself."

Ella sighed. "Have him come around and talk to me about the shutters. We'll see." She checked Solly's dinner plate. He had eaten enough to sustain him. "Solly can have a serving of cobbler now," she told Margaret.

The maid smiled down at the boy as she removed her hands from the sink and shook dishwater off them. "I'll feed it to that baby myself."

Ella carried the tray to the door, put her back to it, and gave it a push.

"David."

"What?"

"Mr. Rainwater's first name," Margaret said. "I figure you wanted to know."

Ella looked at her with annoyance as she backed through the door. When she turned around to face the dining room, her eyes went directly to Mr. Rainwater, who looked up at her. His gaze held hers for a beat before he directed his attention back to Miss Violet, who was telling him about her and Pearl's thrilling days as public school teachers.

"It's so nice to have pleasant conversation with a new acquaintance, isn't it, Sister?" Violet said.

"It is indeed." Pearl simpered, patting her lace collar. "I hope you're with us for a very long time, Mr. Rainwater."

Ella avoided looking at him and kept her expression impassive as she served the dewberry cobbler and cream.

She was sitting at the kitchen table eating her own meal when he poked his head around the edge of the door. Immediately she came to her feet, blotting her mouth. "Mr. Rainwater. Can I get you something?"

He stepped into the kitchen.

Margaret stopped what she was doing and gave him a wide smile. "Coffee's still on."

"No more for me, thank you."

Solly, sitting across from Ella and tapping his spoon against the edge of the table, didn't react.

The new boarder nodded down at Ella's plate. "I wondered when you got to eat."

"Do you need something?"

"Forgive me for interrupting your dinner. I was just wondering if it's all right for me to turn on the porch light so I can read out there."

"Oh, of course. The switch is—"

"I've located the switch. But I wanted to ask before I turned it on."

"Just be sure to turn it off when you come back inside."

He looked at Solly, who was still rhythmically tapping the spoon, then gave Margaret and Ella a nod and backed out the door.

"Nice of him to ax," Margaret said. "That Mr. What's-his-name, the one with the liquor breath? You wouldn't've caught him axing. I hope Mr. Rainwater plans to be with us for a long spell."

Ella sat down and resumed eating.

After Margaret left for home, Ella put Solly to bed, and he fell asleep quickly. She remained kneeling beside his bed, gazing into his sweet face, listening to his soft breathing. When her knees began to ache, she kissed the air just above his cheek and slipped silently from the room, leaving him peacefully sleeping. Nevertheless, she listened for any signs of him stirring as she sat at the kitchen table, shelling black-eyed peas for tomorrow's dinner. It was well after ten o'clock when she made her last inspection of the kitchen and turned out the light.

Her neck and shoulders burned with fatigue as she moved down the darkened hallway. The front porch light was off. Mr. Rainwater hadn't forgotten. But she went to see that he'd also locked the screened door. He hadn't. She reached for the latch.

"If you hook that, I won't be able to get back in."

She jumped at the sound of his voice.

"I'm sorry," he said. "I didn't mean to startle you."

She pushed open the door and stepped out onto the porch. He was sitting in the darkness in one of the wicker chairs. "I'm the one who's sorry," Ella said. "The light was out, so I thought you had come inside. I hate that I disturbed your solitude."

"You didn't. I turned out the light because the bugs attracted to it were becoming a nuisance." He stood up and indicated one of the other chairs. "Join me."

She hesitated for several moments, then moved along the porch and sat down in one of the other chairs.

"The air feels so good I couldn't bring myself to go to my room." He smiled at her. "Even as comfortable as it is."

"I'm glad you like it."

"Cabbage rose wallpaper and all."

They lapsed into a silence broken by the night song of cicadas, a barking dog in the distance, and the faint squeak of the wicker as he repositioned himself in the chair. He stretched his long legs far out in front of him, loosely clasped his hands over the book lying in his lap, and leaned his head back, seeming to be perfectly relaxed.

Ella wasn't sure that such a loose-limbed posture was appropriate when a man and woman, strangers, were alone in the darkness. In fact, she was quite certain it wasn't. It suggested a familiarity that felt vaguely improper, although the chairs in which they were sitting were several yards apart.

"Where was the food going?"

She looked over at him.

"The food that Margaret was packing up when I came into the kitchen," he said. "Where did you send it?"

"To the shantytown. It's on the far east side of town, across the railroad tracks."

He continued to look at her, his eyebrow arched with interest.

"It started out with just a few hoboes who got off the freight trains to camp by the creek. The law ran them off, but more came, and they kept coming, until finally the sheriff gave up trying to keep them away. For the most part they're left alone now. The number fluctuates, but I understand a few hundred are over there at any given time. Whole families. So every few days, I send leftovers, stale bread, overripe fruit. Like that."

"That's very benevolent of you."

She lowered her head, smoothed her hands over her skirt. "It's food I'd have to throw out otherwise."

"I doubt the people in shantytown mind if an apple is bruised."

"In exchange for these scraps, I ask them not to come begging here at the house. Word gets around to newcomers and drifters. Don't go to Barron's Boarding House for a handout. You won't get one."

"Still, you're charitable."

She didn't want him giving her more credit than she deserved. "I don't take it to those poor people myself, Mr. Rainwater. That would be charitable. I send it by Margaret."

"Some people, a lot of people, wouldn't send it at all," he countered in a quiet voice.

She was about to protest further but changed her mind, feeling it would be better to let the subject drop. Another silence fell between them. She sensed that he was more comfortable with it than she was. To her it seemed to stretch out interminably, to the point that she was about to excuse herself and return indoors when he said, "Have you lived here all your life?"

"In this house. My father built it soon after he and my mother married. Several years later, he added on the rooms that Solly and I now share. Except for that addition, the modernized bathrooms and updated kitchen, it's just as it was the day I was born."

"Your parents are dead?"

"Yes."

"Brothers and sisters?"

"I had twin brothers born three years after me. Both died in infancy."

"I'm sorry."

"I can't really remember them." She looked off in the direction of the barking dog, which kept her face averted from him. "Mother and Father never talked about them."

It had been a sorrow that was obviously unbearable to her parents. Neither recovered from it. Overnight, it seemed, her mother had turned into a bitter and cold woman. She no longer smiled, no longer found joy in her healthy daughter, who from then on she kept at arm's length. Ella's father, losing his wife's affection and attention as well as his twin sons, had found his only consolation in whiskey. He'd died of cirrhosis at age forty-five.

Upon his death, her mother had been forced to take in boarders. When she finally succumbed to her sadness—with a great deal of relief, it seemed to Ella—Ella had taken over management of the house. She'd been eighteen. Despite her youth, as prideful as it sounded, she was much better at running the household than her mother had been.

"Murdy told me you're a widow."

She turned and looked at Mr. Rainwater sharply, then almost immediately dropped her gaze. "That's right."

"Unfortunate for you."

She nodded.

"You were left with sole responsibility for Solly."

She raised her head. "He's not a responsibility, Mr. Rainwater. He's a child. My child. A gift."

He retracted his long legs and leaned toward her. "Of course he is. I didn't mean to imply—"

"I'd better go inside." She stood up quickly.

He did likewise.

"Please stop doing that."

"I'm sorry?"

"Stop popping up whenever I stand or enter a room."

"I—"

"I don't expect it. That kind of consideration isn't necessary. I'm your landlady, not your . . . not a . . ." She couldn't think of what she *wasn't* to him, only what she *was*. And what she was didn't warrant his vigilant politeness. "You don't have to stand for me."

"I was taught to stand up for ladies."

"I'm sure you were, but—"

"Habits die hard. But I wouldn't have done it if I'd known it would make you angry."

"I'm not angry."

But her sharp tone indicated otherwise. His eyes penetrated the darkness between them, touched hers, and in fact seemed to see straight through them, making her feel ungracious, uncomfortable, and, somehow, vulnerable.

"Good night, Mr. Rainwater." She turned her back on him and walked to the door, but when she reached for the handle of the screened door, his hand was there first, reaching around her to pull it open. Rather than raise another ruckus about his manners, she went inside. He followed her in, then stood there watching as she went up on tiptoe to latch the door.

"Isn't that hook placed inconveniently high for you?"

"Yes, it's very inconvenient." She hooked the latch, turned to face him. "But it has to be where Solly can't reach it. He wandered off once and was missing for hours before we found him walking on the railroad tracks."

He expelled a long breath, looking regretful. "This is my first night in your house. I've failed to make a good impression."

"You shouldn't be concerned about impressing me, Mr. Rainwater."

"I want you to think well of me."

"I thought well enough of you to rent you the room. Beyond that—"

"You have no opinion of me," he said, finishing for her and further fomenting her irritation with him and the entire conversation.

"That's right, Mr. Rainwater. I don't think too much about

you or about any of my boarders, because, in return, I don't want you thinking too much about me, or Solly, or our circumstances."

He studied her a moment, then said, "You should allow yourself to get angry more often. I think it would do you good."

His candor robbed her of words. Taking umbrage, she just stood there and stared at him.

"Good night, Mrs. Barron." He stepped around her and went upstairs.

FIVE

A week passed. Ella saw little of David Rainwater other than at breakfast and dinner. During mealtimes, he showed remarkable forbearance for the Dunne sisters' chatter and ill-disguised curiosity.

The spinsters began "dressing" for dinner, each night coming downstairs arrayed in their Sunday best, wearing pieces of jewelry and explaining this sudden affectation by asking, rhetorically, what good was having nice things if one never used them? Ella even caught a whiff of cologne one evening and suspected Miss Pearl, who played the coquette whenever in the company of the new boarder.

Mr. Hastings returned one afternoon, barely having time to wash up before dinner. As Ella was serving the salad course, the sisters made the introductions.

"Pleased to meet you, Mr. Rainwater," the salesman said. "It'll be nice to have another man in the house. Do you play chess?"

"Not too well, I'm afraid."

"Excellent! Maybe I can win a game for a change. Ah, Mrs. Barron, I've missed your cooking. Nothing like it where I've been."

"Thank you, Mr. Hastings. Did you have a productive trip?"

"Nothing to boast of, sorry to say. My vendors don't buy what they used to. In fact, nothing even close to what they used to, because they can't sell the inventories they have. Nobody can afford notions these days. People are lucky if they can eat regularly. Despite Mr. Roosevelt's optimistic speeches, times seem to be getting worse, not better."

"Which should make us all the more grateful for our blessings," Miss Violet intoned.

After dinner that night, the two men played chess in the formal parlor while the sisters listened to the radio in the informal parlor. Ella could hear strains of music as she worked in the kitchen. Occasionally she detected a male voice coming from the front room.

Mr. Hastings stayed for two days, then doggedly carried his sample cases down the stairs and out to his car. "I should be back next Tuesday," he informed Ella. "I'll call you if for any reason I'm delayed."

"Have a good trip, Mr. Hastings."

He tipped his hat to her and set off. That evening Mr. Rainwater excused himself immediately after dinner and went up to his room. He hadn't spent any more evenings sitting on the porch, at least none that Ella knew about.

Their encounters were polite, but brief and stilted, as though each was being careful not to offend the other. As she'd requested, he no longer stood up when she entered a room or extended any other overt courtesy. It felt to her as though they had quarreled. They hadn't. Not exactly. But she avoided being alone with him, and he made no attempt to seek her out.

Which was as it should be.

He'd been in residence for two weeks when they had their next private conversation. She'd been cleaning upstairs while Margaret was in the front parlor mending a drapery and watching Solly as he played with spools of thread, which was one of his favorite pastimes.

Ella was toting her basket of cleaning supplies down the stairs when she heard a scraping sound she couldn't identify. She followed it through the kitchen, out the back door, and around the corner of the house.

Mr. Rainwater was applying himself to a garden hoe, using it to chop the dry soil between rows of tomato plants. With his coat and vest draped over a fence post, he was in shirtsleeves, the cuffs rolled to his elbows. Suspenders crisscrossed his back, forming an X over the spot where sweat had plastered his shirt to his skin.

"Mr. Rainwater!"

Her exclamation brought him around. "Mrs. Barron." Resting one arm on the top of the hoe handle, he pushed back his hat and used his sleeve to wipe sweat from his forehead.

"What are you doing?" she asked.

He looked down the handle of the hoe to the freshly tilled soil and uprooted weeds withering in the sun. When he raised his head, he looked at her with the barely contained amusement that was now familiar but no less perturbing. "I'm hoeing the vegetable garden."

His calm statement of the obvious made her even angrier. The weeds he had chopped were evidence that the struggling garden needed attention, but his presumption was untenable. "I was going to weed it myself tomorrow." She glanced up at the blistering afternoon sun. "Early. Before it got too hot."

He chuckled. "It *is* hot. Almost too hot to breathe."

"Which is my point, Mr. Rainwater. Besides doing my work for me, which you shouldn't be, especially not before asking me first, strenuous work like hoeing a garden can't be good for a man in your condition."

His amusement evaporated, and his face became taut, the skin stretched tightly over the prominent bones. "I promise not to drop dead on your tomato plants."

His tone struck her like a slap to the face. She may even have flinched, because immediately he let the hoe drop from beneath his arm and took a step toward her. "I'm sorry." He whipped off his hat and ran his fingers through his hair, pushing it back before replacing his hat. "Please forgive me. That was uncalled for."

She was still too taken aback to speak.

"You think because I took it upon myself to hoe the garden that I'm suggesting you're not competent to do it?" he asked. "Nothing of the sort, Mrs. Barron. I didn't stop to think how you might misread my intentions. In fact, I didn't stop to think at all. It was an impulsive decision, and, the thing is, I didn't do it for you. I did it for me."

She tilted her head up and looked into his face.

"I want and need something to do. I haven't done anything constructive since I moved in, and I dislike the inactivity. It makes the days and nights pass very slowly." He flashed a rueful smile. "You would think I'd welcome the slow passage of time, but I deplore being idle. I want to keep busy and active for as long as I possibly can."

He stared at her for several beats, his aspect intense, as

though he was willing her to understand. Then he released a sigh, his shoulders sagging slightly. He bent down and picked up the hoe. "I'll replace this in the shed."

He retrieved his coat and vest from the fence post and stepped through the rickety chicken-wire gate that sometimes, but rarely, discouraged rabbits from ravaging her garden.

As he walked past her, she said, "I didn't mean to sound so cross."

He stopped and faced her. She was on eye level with his exposed neck, where he'd loosened his tie and unbuttoned his collar button. His skin was slick with sweat. He smelled of its saltiness, of sun and summer heat, of freshly turned loam.

It *was* almost too hot to breathe, she thought. In any case the breath she inhaled seemed insufficient. "My boarders shouldn't do my chores."

"Not even if doing a chore makes one happy?"

She raised her eyes to his.

In a soft voice, he asked, "What's the harm in it, Mrs. Barron?"

"The harm in it is, I don't want any upset of my routine." Sounding desperate, almost afraid, she took a deeper breath before continuing. "If I allowed every boarder to do what he or she pleased, when he or she pleased it, the house would soon be in chaos. I can't let—"

She was shocked into silence when he placed his hand on her shoulder. But before she could fully register that he was actually touching her, she realized his attention was no longer on her. He was looking beyond her. He dropped his things to the ground, at the same time gently, but firmly, pushing her aside and rushing past. "Brother Calvin?"

Ella turned to see the preacher sitting astride a mule. Legs dangling against the animal's sides, Brother Calvin was slumped so far forward, his forehead was almost touching the animal's stiff mane. As she watched in astonishment, he let go of the rope serving as reins, keeled to one side, and slid off the mule onto the ground.

When Mr. Rainwater reached him, he knelt down and gingerly turned the young preacher onto his back. Ella gasped at the sight of the preacher's face. It was bloody and swollen. Mr. Rainwater hissed through his teeth. Ella, reacting to the emergency, did an about-face and ran to the kitchen door. She shouted through the screen for Margaret, then hurried back and dropped to her knees beside the two men.

"What happened to him?"

"Looks to me like he's been beaten," Mr. Rainwater replied.

Brother Calvin was bleeding from several cuts on his face and scalp. His clothing was torn. He was wearing only one shoe. He was conscious, but he was moaning, and his head lolled when Mr. Rainwater slid his arm beneath his shoulders and levered him into a sitting position.

"Help me get him inside," he said to Ella.

The man's size made it an effort. Mr. Rainwater draped one of the preacher's arms across his shoulders, and Ella did the same. Each wedged a shoulder into an armpit, then they managed to heave him up as they struggled to stand. Moving slowly, they half carried, half dragged him to the back steps.

Margaret pushed open the screened door and, upon seeing her beloved minister in that condition, began to shriek.

"Stop that!" Ella ordered. "We need your help. Get his feet."

The maid was struck silent. She clambered down the steps, tucked one of the preacher's feet under each arm, then backed up the steps. All three staggered and stumbled beneath his weight, but they got him through the doorway.

Mr. Rainwater said, "Lower him to the floor."

They did so as gently as possible, but Brother Calvin continued to moan, making Ella fear that his worst injuries were internal. "Get some towels and a washbasin of water," she told Margaret. "And fetch the Mercurochrome from my bathroom. Where's Solly?"

"Right behind you. I was sure to bring him with me when you called."

Solly was sitting on the floor, his back braced against the pantry door, his legs at a right angle to his body. He was staring at his shoes and tapping them together, seemingly unaware of what was taking place.

Ella turned back to Brother Calvin, who groaned when Mr. Rainwater's fingers probed a large lump on his temple. "Should I call Dr. Kincaid?" she asked.

"And the sheriff."

"No!" Brother Calvin's eyes sprang open. In his right one, the black iris floated in a pool of solid red. "No. No, please. No doctor. No sheriff."

As he spoke, he shook his head emphatically, which must have caused him great pain because he squeezed his eyes closed again and groaned. Margaret brought the basin of water. As gently as she could, Ella bathed his wounds with water, then dabbed them with the antiseptic.

Eventually his groans subsided, but he never ceased thanking her for her kindness. Despite his condition, he fretted about the mule.

"What about it?" Ella asked.

"Doesn't belong to me." Between gasps of pain, he told them he was afraid the animal would wander off, so Mr. Rainwater went out to tie it to a fence post, then came back and reassured the preacher that the borrowed mule wasn't going anywhere.

Brother Calvin convinced them he was capable of getting up, so they helped him into a chair at the table. "Do you hurt anywhere inside?" Ella asked him.

"Ribs. A few may be cracked."

"Could you be bleeding internally?"

He shook his head. "No, ma'am. Nothing as bad as that."

But it was bad enough to frighten Miss Violet. She ventured into the kitchen for something, but seeing a bleeding Negro man seated at the table brought her to a dead stop. She pressed an age-spotted hand to her bony chest and cried out, "Oh my!" then quickly backed out.

Whatever was going on, apparently the elderly woman wanted no part of it. Which was just as well with Ella.

Margaret slid a glass of tea within the preacher's reach. He picked it up with both hands and sipped from it. Ella noted that his knuckles were scraped and bloody. He must have landed some hurtful punches of his own.

"What happened? Who did this?" Mr. Rainwater asked. His white shirt was streaked with the other man's blood, but he seemed not to have noticed.

"They were shootin' cows."

"Lord have mercy," Margaret wailed.

"Government men? From the Drought Relief Service?" Mr. Rainwater asked.

The preacher nodded.

"Whose herd was it?" Ella asked.

"Pritchett, his name is."

She looked across at Mr. Rainwater. "George Pritchett. His

family has been operating that dairy farm for at least three generations."

The federal government program had been formulated earlier that year to protect farmers, dairymen, and cattlemen from total ruin. The worst drought in a hundred years had earned the Plains States the nickname of Dust Bowl. Land once farmed or used to graze cattle was now a vast wasteland, ravaged by wind and hordes of insects.

Responding to the worsening emergency, Congress had allocated millions of dollars with which to buy animals from dairy farmers and cattlemen whose herds were literally starving to death. Agents were authorized to pay up to twenty dollars a head, which was far below market value during normal times but better than nothing in the crisis situation.

It seemed a viable program. Livestock deemed healthy enough for consumption was shipped to the Federal Surplus Relief Corporation for slaughtering and processing. The canned meat was then distributed to transient communities, soup kitchens, and breadlines. Farmers and ranchers earned something; hungry people were fed.

But there was also a disquieting aspect to the program. The cattle that weren't culled from herds for meatpacking were destroyed and buried in pits at the point of purchase. It might be a rancher's whole herd or a farmer's single milk cow. While the program had been designed to rescue families suffering the dual effects of the drought and the economic depression, seeing one's lifework destroyed in such a brutal fashion was heart-wrenching.

Brother Calvin continued. "They picked out the fattest ones from the herd—weren't many—and loaded them on a truck. Hauled them off. The ones left, they herded into the bottom of a hole that'd been dug, big as this house. Six of them marksmen lined up along the rim of it.

"Mr. Pritchett went inside the house with his wife and kids and closed the door. He just couldn't bear to watch those cows get shot where they stood. Didn't seem to matter to him that he'd been paid for them. His heart and spirit was broke down."

In the telling of it, the preacher's rolling voice gained strength. It bounced off the walls of the kitchen as though he was in the pulpit warning of hellfire and brimstone. "Then they opened fire. First shots spooked the cows. They's bawling as they dropped. Cows, calves, ever' last one."

It made Ella ill to think of such carnage. Margaret pressed a hand to her trembling lips. Mr. Rainwater's lean jaw was working as though he was grinding his teeth.

Ella said, "I know it's necessary. It's intended to help. But it just seems so cruel."

"Especially to the man who's toiled day and night building a herd," Mr. Rainwater said. "Who beat you up, Brother Calvin? Why?"

The man wiped his eyes with his scratched fist. "Those folks in shantytown heard about what was going to happen out at Mr. Pritchett's place. They came. Coloreds and whites together. Joined up on account of they's all hungry. They came with whatever knifes and hatchets they had. Brought washtubs and cooking pots, thinking they could butcher those cows, get what meat was to be had off those skinny carcasses before it spoiled out there in the sun or was covered up with dirt. Folks that've been living on flour, water, and poke salad greens ain't particular about their cuts of meat."

His eyes began leaking again. "But soon as those government men left, some locals moved in to see that the dead cows didn't get butchered. They's led by a rifle-toting white man with a purple birthmark on his face."

"Conrad."

Mr. Rainwater looked sharply at Ella, who'd spoken the name.

"Conrad Ellis," she said. "He has a birthmark that covers most of his face. A port-wine stain, I think they call it."

"I say it's the mark of Cain," Margaret muttered.

"He's a bully, always has been," Ella said.

"He be meaner than sin."

Ignoring her maid's sneer, Ella went on. "Mr. Ellis, Conrad's father, owns a meatpacking plant. He buys from most of the local ranchers."

"People getting free meat would be bad for his business," Mr. Rainwater remarked. "So he sent his son out there to make sure those folks didn't get any."

Ella frowned. "Conrad wouldn't need an excuse. He enjoys beating up people. He's always spoiling for a fight."

"Especially since—"

"Margaret."

Ella's implied reprimand stopped the maid from saying more, but she looked madder than a hornet as she came to her feet, mumbling, "I'll put some coffee on."

Mr. Rainwater divided a curious look between Ella and Margaret, landing on Ella, who ignored his unspoken questions and returned her attention to Brother Calvin, who was saying, "That white boy was sure enough spoiling for a fight today." He drained his glass of tea and carefully set it on the table.

"Soon as those government shooters cleared out, those shantytown people, me with them, ran down into that hole and started butchering those cows. Long as they were dead anyway, they could feed folks. Tonight. Not wait till the government got around to distributing canned meat. That was my thinking. And Mr. Pritchett's, too, I guess, 'cause him and his wife come back outside and were passing out kitchen knives to anybody who didn't have one.

"Then those boys roared up in a pickup truck, blaring the horn and shooting off firearms. They spilled out the back of that truck, waving baseball bats and rifles and yelling for those folks to scatter. When nobody paid them any mind but kept on hacking off pieces of those cows, they began knocking heads with the bats and the butts of their rifles. Men, kids, women, didn't matter."

"Where was the law?"

"The sheriff and a carload of deputies were there. Watching, but doing nothing till Mr. Pritchett took up a shotgun. He was shouting at those boys to get off his place and leave those poor shantytown folks alone, that all they wanted was meat that was gonna go to waste. Sheriff told him to put down that fool shotgun before he killed somebody."

Here the preacher began shaking his head and weeping more copiously. "I saw this myself. That mean one with the birthmark went up on the porch and yanked a little boy straight out of Mrs. Pritchett's arms. Couldn't've been more than two or three years old. He threatened to bash that child's skull in if Mr. Pritchett didn't lay down his shotgun and let him and his buddies get on with the business of making sure the government program went off like it was s'pposed to."

"Christ."

The minister looked at Mr. Rainwater with soulful eyes. "The Lord forgives you the blasphemy, Mr. Rainwater. It was an awful sight. Dreadful in His eyes, too." He wiped tears from his eyes again. "I don't think Mr. Roosevelt had this in mind, do you? Anyhow, seeing his wife goin' all hysterical, and his baby boy's life threatened, that well-meaning Mr. Pritchett just give up.

"He dropped down on the steps of his porch and watched as those mean boys chased hungry folks back to shantytown. All he could do was sit there and cry over that bloody mess left in his pasture. He'd seen most of those cows born, probably helped pull some of them out of their mamas. To see 'em just shot like that, then wasted . . ." The preacher lost his will to continue.

When he stopped speaking, the only noises in the kitchen were those of the burbling percolator on the stove and Solly tapping his shoes together. Finally Ella asked, "What happens now?"

"They'll be buried."

Brother Calvin agreed to Mr. Rainwater's explanation with a nod. "There were front loaders parked down the road from the farm, ready to roll, fill back up the hole they'd dug." He shook his head sorrowfully. "I know men have gotta get whatever work they can. But I don't know that I could ever hire on to shoot dumb cows and their calves. I don't know that I could bury their carcasses in a pit while hungry children, within shouting distance, were crying and needing supper tonight."

Mr. Rainwater leaned across the table toward him. "You were trying to help the shantytown people and got caught in the fray?"

"That's right. I go down there sometimes and hold services for those folks," he explained. "I encouraged them to be ready when those shooters went out to the Pritchett farm. I promised them meat. At least a bone for a soup pot. I didn't count on men threatening to brain little boys with baseball bats." His massive shoulders shook as he began to weep in earnest. "I feel responsible for ever' blow struck."

Ella laid a comforting hand on his forearm. "You're not to blame, Brother Calvin. You were trying to help." She looked across at Mr. Rainwater. "You know Dr. Kincaid better than I do. Do you think he would go to shantytown, treat those people with the worst injuries? I can't ask him to do that, but you're his kin."

He stood up and began rolling down his shirtsleeves. "I'll go now."

"Stop back here before you leave for shantytown. Margaret and I will gather some things."

He nodded as he left through the back door.

Ella was waiting for them when Mr. Rainwater returned a half hour later with Dr. Kincaid. "I need some help," she called from the front porch.

The two men carried boxes of food, clothing, and household items from the house and loaded them into Mr. Rainwater's car. "You did all this in the brief time I was gone?" he asked as he hefted a flour sack filled with clothing that Solly had outgrown.

"I've been collecting it for a while, waiting for the right time to give it away."

While the men were stowing the last of the things in the car, Ella rushed back into the kitchen, asking Margaret to keep a close eye on Solly and promising to return in time to serve dinner. Then she grabbed her hat and went running out the front door. "Wait, I'm coming."

"That isn't necessary, Mrs. Barron," the doctor said. He was sweating profusely.

"I know it isn't necessary, but I can help."

"Maybe Margaret would be better suited—"

"Margaret is a Negro, Dr. Kincaid. I don't want to put her in danger of reprisal from a group of bigoted hoodlums. They enjoy bullying. They like it even better when their victims are colored people."

The doctor looked toward Mr. Rainwater for reinforcement, but Mr. Rainwater took her side. "You can't argue with that, Murdy."

The doctor clapped his hat on his head. "Let's go, then. Mrs. Kincaid is having a hissy fit as it is. She swore to send the law out looking for me if I wasn't back in an hour."

But an hour wasn't near enough time to see everyone who had sustained an injury in the melee at the Pritchetts' farm.

Ella and Mr. Rainwater doled out aspirin tablets and consolation to those with minor injuries, while the doctor treated the worst of them. He set the bones of grim-faced men who swigged moonshine to brace themselves against the pain. He bound bleeding wounds. He stitched what gashes he could with his limited supplies, then smeared antiseptic salves over the rest when his suturing threads ran out. He helped birth a stillborn baby from a woman who tiredly said it was a shame her child was dead but she couldn't have fed another mouth anyhow. His little soul was better off in heaven, she said.

When all the wounded were treated, Ella and Mr. Rainwater circulated among the rickety lean-tos, patched tents, pasteboard boxes, and rusty cars serving as shelters. They passed out clothing, cast-off household items, and foodstuffs they'd brought. The eyes of the people looking back at Ella were either apathetic toward her generosity or pathetically grateful for it. She found both reactions equally disturbing.

When she'd given away everything she was carrying with her, she picked her way through the encampment back to Dr. Kincaid, who was giving instructions to the woman whose baby had been born dead.

He backed away from her bed, which was the lid of a box that she'd dragged into the shade of a pecan tree, and placed his hands in the small of his back as he straightened up. He'd left his suit jacket and hat in the car. His shirt was dirty and damp with perspiration. There was a smear of blood on his sleeve.

"We've done a little good, I think," he remarked.

"Not enough."

"No. Never enough." He smiled at Ella grimly. "All the same, we'd better be on our way before Mrs. Kincaid sends out a posse."

"Will there be any pain?" Ella asked him.

"Not much, no. The child was small, only seven months along. As births go, it was reasonably easy."

But then he realized that Ella wasn't talking about the woman who'd lost her newborn. She was looking at Mr. Rainwater, who was shaking hands with a man dressed only in grimy overalls. At each of the man's legs was a grubby, barefoot child, clinging to the dirty denim of his daddy's pants with hands that were even dirtier. The man was holding a third child in his arms. Ella had heard him telling Mr. Rainwater that his wife had died of tuberculosis a week ago, and that he didn't know how he was going to look for work and take care of his children at the same time.

She was too far away to hear what the two were saying to each other now, but she imagined that Mr. Rainwater was telling him not to lose hope. He released the man's hand, tousled the hair of one of the children, and turned to make his way back to her and the doctor.

She looked at Dr. Kincaid, her question hovering between them.

"Yes," he said.

A shudder passed through her. She swallowed dryly. "Can you give him something for it?"

"When he asks for it, yes."

"Will he? Ask."

The doctor watched his kinsman winding his way around campfires and huddles of people. "Yes, Mrs. Barron," the doctor replied bleakly. "He will."

SIX

The Sunday following the incident at the Pritchetts' farm, someone driving a pickup truck threw a bottle through a window of the AME church during the evening worship service. The bottle narrowly missed striking an elderly woman who was sitting on the end of the pew nearest the window, but beyond shattering a large pane of glass, it did no other harm. Leaving a wake of shouted racial slurs and a cloud of dust, the pickup sped away.

Brother Calvin's melodious voice kept his congregation under control. None of the women panicked, none of the men went after the pickup. When the frightened children had been quieted, Brother Calvin continued his sermon and, by the conclusion of the service, had added ten converts to his flock.

The preacher's face still looked battered, but the cuts on it and one cracked rib were the extent of his injuries. Miss Violet Dunne's take on the minister's participation in the incident at the Pritchetts' farm was "He's lucky they didn't lynch him."

Although Ella's position on racial matters differed greatly from the spinster's, she did agree with that summation. She felt that Brother Calvin had been fortunate to escape with his life.

It was first believed that the attack on the church was racially motivated, a warning to coloreds not to meddle in concerns that were basically reserved for whites, like government issues. That general opinion changed when, the very next night, two tents in shantytown went up in flames and a bag of horse manure was dumped into the creek from which the people who camped there drew their water.

It seemed the prevailing bigotry extended to poor whites and hoboes, too.

But after those incidents, Conrad Ellis and his crowd apparently lost interest in organized terrorism. They reverted to their customary forms of mischief making—reckless driving, public intoxication, and behaving obnoxiously at every opportunity.

The mass grave at the Pritchett farm was barely noticeable from the road, and lye prevented the odor of decay from fouling the air, but the incident was still fresh on everyone's mind. Other dairy farmers and cattlemen in the region were selling their herds to the FSRC's agents, but none of those transactions had sparked incidents, partially because they had taken place in rural areas, not in the immediate vicinity of Gilead and its shantytown full of people who were barely subsisting.

In order to avoid foreclosure of their property, many local landowners were eager to take advantage of the government program before the money allotted to buy cattle ran out. Sentiment extended only so far when it came to a choice between losing a herd and losing everything.

No one blamed a man for trying to make the most of a dire situation. Many townsfolk admired Mr. Pritchett, who had denounced Sheriff Anderson for standing by and doing nothing when the ruffians turned a terrible situation into a life-threatening melee. Others were outspoken in their contempt for Mr. Ellis and his ilk, who would actually profit from the program while cattlemen and farmers were left with nothing with which to rebuild. Some, those who disliked the shanty-town and distrusted everybody in it, thought the vagrants had got no better than they deserved.

Rumors spread rampantly. Backbiting turned vicious. Tempers were short and tension was high. Everyone seemed to be waiting for something bad to happen. Dread was as oppressive as the unrelenting heat.

One evening as he studied the chessboard, waiting for Mr. Rainwater to make his move, Mr. Hastings absently remarked, "Sticky today."

Mr. Rainwater limited his response to an absentminded nod.

Ella had been baking all day, so even after the sun went down, the kitchen remained a hotbox. There wasn't a breeze to be found, although every window in the house was open in the hope that one would be coaxed inside. She had asked the gentlemen if they minded her and Solly sharing the front parlor with them, where the small electric fan at least stirred the sultry air.

Mr. Hastings had answered for both of them. "Of course not."

She'd settled into a chair and situated Solly on the floor beside her, where he played with spools of thread while she caught up on mending.

Mr. Hastings took a sip from his sweating glass of iced tea and, continuing his one-sided conversation, said, "Humid as it is, it could storm before daybreak. Dare I think we might actually see rain?"

Mr. Rainwater thoughtfully moved a chess piece. "If I didn't know better," he said slowly, "I'd think you were trying to distract me with all this talk of the weather."

"Guilty," the older man said around a chuckle. "I'm trying to hold on to my title and my dignity. You're improving with each game."

"But you still outplay me."

"Not for long, is my guess."

Mr. Rainwater smiled across at him, but Ella also caught his gaze shifting to Solly, who was absorbed in his play with the wooden spools. For the past half hour, she had become aware that Mr. Rainwater spent as much time studying Solly as he did the chessboard. Solly had been playing quietly, but it suddenly occurred to her that he might be a distraction, preventing her boarders from fully enjoying their game.

Hastily she snipped the thread she'd been using to sew a button back onto one of Solly's shirts. She replaced her thimble, thread, and scissors in the sewing basket. Carefully she pushed her needle into a stiff white card and slipped it into an inside pocket of the basket.

Mr. Rainwater, noticing, asked, "Are you finished?"

"For tonight."

Mr. Hastings came around in his seat. "Are you leaving us, Mrs. Barron? I was enjoying your company."

She smiled wanly, grateful to him for the polite lie. "It's time I put Solly to bed."

She bent down to gather up the spools of thread that he'd been playing with. He protested when she wrested one from his hand and dropped it into the basket. "Time for bed, Solly," she said, praying he would go without creating a scene.

Her prayer was in vain.

Solly began the high-pitched whine that signaled he was

distressed. He raised his hands to the sides of his head and began flapping them against his ears, as the whine intensified into a full-blown screech.

Leaving her sewing basket on the floor beside her chair, Ella picked him up and wrapped her arms around him in an effort to pin his waving hands and kicking feet to her body.

"I apologize for the interruption, gentlemen. Good night."

Carrying Solly, she practically ran from the room. As she passed the staircase, an apparition in a lightweight robe and a hairnet leaned over the railing from the gallery above and called down, "Is everything all right?"

"Fine, Miss Pearl. Good night."

Ella rushed into her bedroom and fell against the door to close it, hoping the heavy oak would block the terrible sound issuing from her little boy. She clutched him to her, shushing him, whispering a litany of comforting words, yet knowing the uselessness of them. He was tortured by demons against which she was powerless. To her and others, his fits were a disruption. To him, they were sheer torment, the extent of which she couldn't even conceive. She couldn't protect him from his own mind, couldn't protect him from an unseen enemy, and that was her greatest heartache.

Each time something like this happened, it also increased her fear that she wouldn't be able to protect Solly from being institutionalized. What if Mr. Rainwater reported this episode to Dr. Kincaid? What if the doctor took matters into his own hands and notified authorities of the dangers Solly's fits posed?

Short of that, if this continued to happen, she might lose boarders. Kind as they were, there was a limit to their tolerance for these outbursts. Times were hard, money was scarce, and every penny counted. She couldn't afford to lose good, permanent boarders like the spinster sisters or Mr. Hastings, especially since Mr. Rainwater's residency was temporary.

After catching her breath, she carried Solly into the small room in which he slept. Closing the door made the room even hotter and more airless than it already was, but the door would remain closed until she got him calmed down.

But nothing she did stopped his hand flapping or his squeal, made even more earsplitting as it echoed in the small room. In the end, she left him long enough to rush back into the formal parlor and, ignoring the anxious and inquisitive eyes of the two men, retrieved her sewing basket. When she returned to Solly's bedroom, she upturned the basket onto his bed, spilling the contents onto it.

He stopped screeching instantly. Picking out two spools of thread, he set them carefully on the floor beside his bed, close to touching but not quite. Then, one by one, he replaced the items scattered across his bed in the basket. When he was done, he set the basket on the floor, climbed up onto his bed, lay his head on the pillow, and closed his eyes. He was asleep within seconds.

Ella fell back against the wall and slid down it until she was sitting on the floor. She was damp with perspiration and more exhausted than she would have been if she'd run all the way to Brownsville and back.

Bending her head low, she picked the pins from her hair, relieving the back of her neck from the weight of the tight bun. There was also relief in Solly's silence and inactivity, and for that she felt very ashamed. She looked into the sleeping face of her son, and her heart constricted with love and a twinge of pity. She had no way of knowing, but she wondered if perhaps sleep was the only state in which he found his own peace.

She scooted across the floor on her bottom to the side of the bed, being careful not to disturb the two spools of thread that Solly had so painstakingly placed. For several minutes, she simply stared at him with that same mix of love and sorrow. Then, gently, she touched his hand where it lay on the counterpane. Her fingertips traced the fine blue network of veins just beneath his pale skin. Barely making contact, she ran her finger across his eyelashes, then along the rim of his ear.

He didn't flinch or deflect her touch. He didn't even stir except for the almost indiscernible rise and fall of his thin chest. These were the moments of her life most precious to her, when she could luxuriate in touching her child without being rebuffed. During the hours that others slept in her house, she often spent in this tiny cell of a room that had bars on its only window to prevent escape. She passed many dark nights caressing Solly, imagining a day when he would look at her and smile with recognition and reciprocated love.

It was a ridiculous hope. Many had told her so. But she clung to it nonetheless. If ever she let it go, she feared falling into an abyss of despair from which there would be no escape.

Only one clap of thunder preceded the rain. It didn't start with a few sprinkles and build. It fell suddenly and violently, an instant downpour.

In a heartbeat, Ella was up. She grabbed her robe and was still pushing her arms into the sleeves of it as she left her room. The central hallway was dark, but flashes of lightning provided intermittent illumination as she rushed toward the formal parlor.

When she stepped into the room, a lightning bolt momentarily blinded her. Carefully, she felt her way across the room to the west wall, where the tall windows remained open. Rain had already doused the sills. Her bare feet discovered the floor wet and slippery. Quickly, she closed the corner window and moved to the next.

She made her way down the row, shutting out the pelting rain. Jagged bolts of lightning opened up cracks in the black sky. Treetops were tossed by an angry wind. Someone's laundry had been ripped off the clothesline and was being blown down the street, empty pants and shirts tumbling like circus performers.

When the last window had been closed, she left the twin parlors and went to the front door. It was on the south side of the house and protected by the second-story balcony, but rain had been wind-driven across the porch and through the screen. The wind was so strong she felt resistance when she closed the solid door against it. She flipped the lock to secure it, rested against it for a moment, then turned.

He was standing on the bottom tread of the staircase, his right hand on the newel post, as though he'd been arrested in motion when he saw her.

He all but disappeared during the intervals of darkness between blinding flashes of bluish light when his shirt showed up abnormally white. Only one button in the center of his chest was done up. He hadn't taken time to tuck in his shirttail. His suspenders formed loops against his thighs. His feet were bare.

Ella knew she must look as disheveled as he, maybe more so. Her hair was wildly curling around her face, a tangled mane down her back. Her robe was damp from rain. The wet hem of it clung to her ankles. Her feet felt cold and clammy, reminding her she was barefoot.

All this registered with her in a matter of seconds, during which it seemed that her breath had been snatched from her body. A lightning bolt struck dangerously close. The thunder that followed shook the house. Glassware and china made tinkling sounds inside cabinetry. The light fixture above the hallway rattled. The back door slammed shut, echoing the thunderclap.

Even then, neither of them moved. Their eyes stayed locked. Ella's heart felt on the verge of bursting.

She said hoarsely, "The storm finally broke."

He held her stare for several moments longer, slowly shaking his head. "No. It didn't."

She drew in a tremulous breath, her heart crowding her lungs, and forced her feet to move.

As she went past him toward her room, he added quietly, "Not yet."

As soon as breakfast had been served and the kitchen cleaned, she and Margaret went outside to clear up the debris left by the storm. Ella was surprised to find Brother Calvin gathering broken tree limbs and heaping them into a pile in the ditch that ran along her property line.

She looked at Margaret accusingly, but her maid shrugged. "I didn't send for him."

"That's true, Mrs. Barron. I came on my own, hoping to help out."

She had relented and let him paint the shutters. He'd also been paid to do other chores that required more strength and time than she had. "I can't afford another employee," she told him now, even as he sawed a broken limb from the pecan tree.

"No charge. I owe you."

"You don't—"

"We're a long way from even, Mrs. Barron."

When the damaged limb fell free from the tree trunk, he turned and looked at her. She saw that the white of one of his eyes still had a spot of red in it. Realizing that this was a matter of honor to him, she assented with a small nod. "I appreciate your help, Brother Calvin."

"That storm was all bluster. Ground's hardly damp."

Ella had heard on the radio that morning that rainfall amounts were barely measurable and that what little rain there had been had fallen so quickly that it ran off before it could soak into the hard-baked ground. It certainly hadn't put an end to the drought.

The preacher motioned toward the ditch. "Later today, I'll burn this brush for you. There's more to add to the pile."

"Come to the kitchen at lunchtime. Margaret will feed you."

"Your butter beans?"

She smiled. "Not today."

"Whatever it is, I thank you, ma'am."

Ella was busy for the rest of the morning, seeing to it that all the windowsills and floors that had been rained on the night before were mopped and dried. Her parlor draperies were damp. She shook them out and turned the fan on them to speed up the drying process.

The noon meal was served, but she had so many chores to catch up on, she turned that meal over to Margaret, then sent her to the store with a long shopping list. By midafternoon, Ella had pork chops braising on the stove and was putting finishing touches on a banana pudding when she realized that Solly was no longer in the kitchen with her.

"Solly!" She burst out of the kitchen and raced down the center hallway toward the front door, through which he'd ventured out once before.

"In here."

She turned abruptly and retraced her steps, stopping when

she reached the arched opening into the informal parlor. Mr. Rainwater was sitting on the floor, a set of dominoes scattered in front of him. Beside him was Solly, watching intently as Mr. Rainwater picked up a domino and stood it on end in perfect alignment with the previous one.

"What—"

"Ssh. He's okay. Watch."

Any other time, she would resent being shushed, but she was so intrigued by Solly's apparent concentration, she stepped into the room and lowered herself onto the nearest chair, perching right on the edge of the seat.

Mr. Rainwater continued to add dominoes to the snaking line he had formed on the hardwood floor. Solly's eyes followed every careful motion of his hands.

"I noticed last night how he was playing with the spools. Stacking them, placing them in perfect juxtaposition." Although Mr. Rainwater was speaking to Ella, he didn't look up at her. His concentration on placing the dominoes just so was as intense as Solly's. "Seeing that gave me this idea."

To prevent any false impressions, she said quietly, "He does that with other things, Mr. Rainwater. Toothpicks. Buttons. Bottle caps. Anything uniform in shape."

Rather than dim his enthusiasm, which she had expected, her statement seemed to validate his optimism. "Really?" Smiling, he continued to add to the column of dominoes. Solly remained transfixed. He seemed not to notice that his knee was touching Mr. Rainwater's.

When all the dominoes had been placed, Mr. Rainwater withdrew his hands and then sat motionless.

Solly stared at the line of dominoes for the better part of a minute before he extended his index finger to the last one in the line, and nudged it. It toppled, creating a contagion until all were down.

Ella stood up. "Thank you for watching him."

Mr. Rainwater raised his hand, palm out. "Wait." Moving slowly, he stretched out his hands and began to turn the dominoes over so that they lay with the dots down. Then he shuffled them as though he was about to start a game. When they were all spread out, he sat back again. "Your turn, Solly."

The boy sat, staring at the dominoes for a long time before he reached for one and stood it on its end.

Ella knew that her son had responded not to his name but to his mysterious inner urging to line up the dominoes. It was that trait, his insistence on uniformity and order, and his violent outbursts if things weren't in that particular order, that had first signaled her that he was different from other children. Normal children left their playthings helter-skelter.

"He wasn't always like he is now."

Mr. Rainwater looked up at her.

"He was a perfectly normal baby," she continued. "He nursed and slept on schedule. He cried only when he was wet or hungry or sleepy. The rest of the time, he was content. He reacted normally to voices and sounds. He recognized me and his father, Margaret, the boarders who were living here then. We played patty-cake and peekaboo. He laughed. He crawled at nine months and walked at thirteen. He was just like every other baby. Even exceptional, I think, because I had him toilet trained soon after he turned two, which is early for any child, but especially for boys. So I'm told."

She looked down and realized that she was clutching her apron with both hands. She forced her fists to relax and let go, then smoothed out the wrinkles she'd made in the fabric.

"But during his twos, when most children are asserting their independence and revealing their personalities, Solly seemed to . . . to retreat. He stopped responding when we tried to play games with him. Once his attention was focused on something, we couldn't draw it away, and he became very distressed when we tried.

"His interest in and awareness of what was going on around him decreased. His fits became more frequent. The rocking, the hand flapping became constant. For a time, I could stop him, but then each day my sweet, smart baby boy slipped a little bit farther away from me." She lifted her gaze from her lap to Solly, who was still lining up the dominoes. "Until he disappeared entirely." She looked at Mr. Rainwater and raised her shoulder. "I never got him back."

He'd listened without moving. Now he looked down at Solly. "Murdy thinks he should be placed in a facility."

Immediately regretting that she'd made an exception to her usual reticence and had spoken so openly to him, she went on the defensive. "The two of you discussed my child?"

"I asked him why Solly is the way he is."

"Why?"

"Why did I ask? I wanted to know."

"Mr. Rainwater, your curiosity is—"

"Not curiosity, concern."

"Why should you be concerned about a boy who, up till a few weeks ago, you didn't even know existed?"

"Because the first time I saw him, he'd pulled a pan of hot starch onto himself."

Would she have preferred that he not be concerned about a child who'd burned himself? No. Nevertheless, his interest offended her. She'd thought he was different from gawking strangers. He wasn't. He was merely too well mannered to ask rude questions and stare with flagrant fascination or repugnance. He was too polite to point and laugh, make jokes, say cruel things. But going behind her back and discussing Solly with the doctor was equally contemptible.

"If you wanted to know about Solly, why didn't you ask me?"

"Because I sensed that you would react exactly as you are."

His reasonable tone only emphasized how uneven hers was. She couldn't help but wonder what else the doctor had told him about her. It was infuriating, the two of them talking about her. She felt heat rising out of her collar, up her neck, and into her face.

As though reading her mind, he said, "We weren't gossiping, Mrs. Barron. I asked Murdy a few questions, and he explained."

"Did he enlist you to persuade me to put Solly away, since all his attempts have failed?"

"No."

"I will never have Solly locked up in an institution."

He nodded, whether in agreement with her position or in understanding of it she couldn't tell. "That's a very courageous decision." The statement was just as ambivalent as his nod.

She stood. "It will be dinnertime soon. I have work to do." She knelt down beside Solly, ready to pick him up and, even if he pitched one of his fits, carry him from the room and away from Mr. Rainwater.

To her consternation, her boarder laid a hand on her arm. "Please. Look. Tell me what you notice."

Solly had finished lining up all the dominoes and was staring at the serpentine row. As she watched, he gently poked the one at the end. It took only seconds for them to topple just as they had before.

Missing Mr. Rainwater's point, she looked at him inquisitively.

He said, "Notice the dots."

It took only a few seconds for her to see what he wanted her to, and when she did, gooseflesh broke out on her arms. Her heart hitched. She made a small, involuntary sound of astonishment.

The dominoes had been scattered on the floor, facedown. Yet Solly had selected them one by one and lined them up in numerical order, from the double blank to the double six.

Her breath coming quickly, she turned to Mr. Rainwater. "How did you teach him to do that?"

His smile widened. "I didn't."

SEVEN

"They're called idiot savants."

It was the day following the discovery of Solly's remarkable ability. Last evening after dinner, Ella and Mr. Rainwater had tested him several times. He never failed to place the dominoes in ascending order, even though he selected them while they were lying facedown.

That morning, as soon as breakfast was over, Ella dispatched Margaret to the doctor's office with a note briefly describing what had taken place the night before and asking if she could bring Solly in for a consultation.

She purposely didn't use the telephone to communicate with the doctor, mistrusting the operator, who was notorious for listening in on conversations. Until she had an explanation for Solly's rare talent, she didn't want town gossips whispering about it.

People tended to fear anyone who was different. Some were

particularly narrow-minded in their regard of simpletons, believing they should be isolated for the welfare and safekeeping of themselves and others.

From her childhood, Ella remembered a mongoloid man named Dooley. He was harmless, actually sweet and friendly. But he lacked the discretion that came from conditioning, and his overt friendliness made some people uncomfortable.

He wandered into a widow lady's yard one day, Ella believed innocently, and happened to look into her bedroom window while she was undressed. She raised a hue and cry, and Dooley was sent away to a hospital for the insane in East Texas. He died there.

Ella harbored an ongoing fear that mandatory institutionalization would be Solly's fate, too. One act, like poor Dooley's innocent window peeping, could cause Solly to be taken from her and put away. So she safeguarded him diligently, knowing it would take only one incident to turn a tide of suspicion and fear against her son.

Dr. Kincaid had sent back a message with Margaret that he would see them at three o'clock, which was after regular office hours. Mr. Rainwater had asked if he could accompany them, and Ella had consented. It had been he, after all, who had discovered Solly's ability. They rode to town in his car.

They'd been shown into a cramped office by Mrs. Kincaid, who told them that the doctor would be with them shortly. She'd offered them something to drink, but both had declined, although Ella had accepted a candy stick for Solly. They'd been waiting only a minute or two when the doctor came in, bringing a box of dominoes with him.

Ella felt her pulse rise when Mr. Rainwater went through the ritual of shuffling and turning the dominoes facedown on the doctor's scarred desktop. But Solly performed as he had the day before. Dr. Kincaid shook his head in wonderment, then leaned back in his squeaky chair and made that startling and offensive statement.

"Idiot savant?" Ella repeated.

Correctly reading her negative reaction, he said, "It's a disagreeable term, I know. But until the medical community comes up with a better one, that's the name for this particular anomaly."

"Anomaly," she said, testing the word. "What is it, precisely?"

"*Precisely,* no one knows." Dr. Kincaid motioned down to the medical book on his desk, which was opened to a page of finely printed text. "Are you familiar with the term IQ, intelligence quotient? It's a relatively new term referring to the measurement of one's mental capacity."

She and Mr. Rainwater said they'd heard of it.

"Today we would deem a person with an IQ of twenty or below uneducably mentally retarded. But for centuries, someone with that limited a capacity was known as an idiot." The doctor slid on a pair of reading glasses and consulted the text. "Late in the nineteenth century a German doctor studied individuals with classic mental retardation, either from birth or resulting from injury, who also possessed uncanny, even miraculous skills. Usually they were extraordinary mathematical, musical, or memory-related talents. He combined the term for people with extremely low intelligence with the French word for an extremely learned individual and derived the term *idiot savant.*"

"And that's what Solly is?" Although Ella found the term objectionable, she was eager to know more.

Dr. Kincaid removed his eyeglasses. "I don't know that for

certain, Mrs. Barron. I'm just a country town doctor. I've heard about idiot savants, but until your note described to me what Solly did yesterday with the dominoes, I had very little knowledge of the classification. I looked it up in preparation for this visit.

"And frankly," he continued ruefully, "I'm still largely in the dark. My research didn't yield much. Information on the subject is scarce and often contradictory. Only a handful of doctors in the world have treated such patients, and even they don't know why those patients have such disparate characteristics.

"In fact, no one has provided a definitive explanation of how this anomaly occurs, or why. Does something happen in the womb while the brain is being formed, or is it postnatal in origin? Does it occur as a result of head trauma, emotional impact, or environment?" He shrugged.

Ella hesitated, then said, "Rarely a day goes by that I don't ask myself if Solly is this way because of something I did, or didn't do, either before he was born, or after." It was a hard admission to make. Dr. Kincaid gave her a gentle smile.

"I can almost assure you no, Mrs. Barron. If it happened in the womb, it was an unavoidable accident of nature. I assisted you with his birth, and nothing out of the ordinary happened. If, when he was an infant, Solly had suffered an injury or illness severe enough to cause brain damage, you would have known it.

"The theories concerning the causes of his condition are so widely varied that none have substance. At least not in my opinion. But if I were forced to guess, I would say that it happens as the fetus is forming but isn't necessarily manifested in infancy."

"Solly was developing as other children do."

Dr. Kincaid laid his hand on the open text. "It's a matter of record that symptoms generally begin showing up around the age Solly was when you started noticing them."

Mr. Rainwater spoke for the first time. "Bizarre. That brilliant medical men can't pinpoint the cause."

The doctor said, "When they can't explain an aberration, they often relegate it to the supernatural. Some theorize that this condition is spiritual in nature, that idiot savants have a direct pipeline to God's mind. They speculate that people like Solly think on an entirely different plane from you and me, which is why they're often unaware of their surroundings, other people, or any stimuli." Again, the doctor smiled at Ella. "It might be comforting for you to believe that Solly is special because he communes directly with God and angels."

"I don't want to be comforted, Dr. Kincaid. I want to be educated on Solly's potential, and what kind of life he can have. I want to know what I must do to give him every possible chance of reaching that potential."

She looked at her son where he sat, rocking back and forth from his waist up, picking at a button on his shirt and sucking on the candy stick, locked inside a realm she couldn't breach. Mr. Rainwater asked the question forming in her mind.

"Do these people ever recover, Murdy? With help, can they lead normal lives?"

Dr. Kincaid consulted the open textbook again, but Ella thought he was buying time, not really seeking an answer to the question.

"The documented cases wouldn't fill a thimble. The criteria for the diagnosis are constantly under debate and continually changing. The only thing these cases have in common is that there's little commonality. Each individual is different. Their symptoms and the severity of them vary. Some do learn language skills. They can communicate on a limited basis. But they rarely apply their superior knowledge to any practical use."

Mr. Rainwater asked him to elaborate.

The doctor thought for a moment. "For instance, an individual who has demonstrated amazing powers of recall might read one of Shakespeare's plays once and be able to quote it verbatim. He doesn't do that for any reason other than because he can. He doesn't memorize the play because he wants to learn it by heart. He doesn't read it because he's curious about the story's outcome. He has no interest in the material whatsoever. The words would mean no more to him than the listings in the phone book. If he reads it, he knows it. It's not something he seeks to do for enlightenment or entertainment."

"But he *can* read Shakespeare," Ella said.

The doctor must have detected her hopeful inflection, and seemed unhappy about dispelling it. "Some like Solly do read, Mrs. Barron, that's true. Others don't read, speak, or communicate on any level, while, miraculously, they can play difficult compositions on the piano after hearing them only once. Some are as withdrawn as Solly, even resistant to being touched, as he is. Yet they can solve highly complicated mathematical problems instantly, when it would take even a gifted mathematician days to work them out." He raised his hands, palms up.

"The truth is, I'm delighted that you've discovered Solly's special gift. But I can't explain it or speculate on how beneficial it will be to him. I wouldn't dare give you false hope that he'll eventually acquire language skills. I simply don't know, Mrs. Barron. And I fear that no one else does, either."

Dr. Kincaid's summary of Solly's condition should have dampened Ella's excitement over his incredible skill, but she didn't let it. She considered this a tremendous milestone in her attempts to reach her son. It represented to her a small crack in the wall behind which his mind and personality were barricaded.

Having found that small chink, she set her mind to prying it wider, wide enough, she hoped, for her to squeeze through. Her heart's desire was to have some channel of communication between them, no matter how narrow.

Each day, she stole time away from her housekeeping chores to spend with him. Replicating the dots on dominoes, she drew sets of dots on paper, then handed the pencil to Solly, hoping he would draw his own groups of dots and from there learn that a set of dots represented a particular number, and that numbers could be added and subtracted to make other numbers.

But he never took hold of the pencil or showed any interest in drawing dots on paper. When she covered his hand with hers and tried to guide the pencil, he threw a tantrum. Banging his head against hers, he caused a bruise on her chin that was visible for days. For the time being, she gave up on trying to get him to draw dots and went back to the dominoes. The game kept Solly pacified and kept her hopeful for another breakthrough.

One evening Solly was seated on the kitchen floor lining up the dominoes while she folded towels and washcloths. Mr. Rainwater came in to return a used coffee cup.

He remarked, "I see Solly hasn't lost interest."

"No. But he hasn't advanced, either." She explained her frustration over her son's failure to understand that he could draw domino dots on paper. "I was hoping he would come to understand that the dots represent a number, and that numbers mean something."

"Maybe he does understand that. If he didn't, why would he always put the dominoes in order?"

She had no answer for that.

"Would you mind if I worked with him?" he asked.

"Doing what?"

He raised a shoulder. "I don't know yet. I'll have to think about it."

The vagueness of his reply made her uneasy. She was about to say no to his request when she remembered the many kindnesses he had extended to Solly. He seemed to have a genuine and unselfish interest in him. He was also inordinately patient, and working with Solly required tremendous patience, which sometimes even she lacked. She also was thinking about the day in the garden when he was hoeing up weeds for lack of something better to do. Mr. Rainwater needed to feel useful.

She consented, but with a condition. "If Solly becomes anxious—"

"I'll stop whatever we're doing. I promise."

Three days later, she came in from outside, her apron full of tomatoes and yellow squash she'd picked in the garden. Margaret was peeling potatoes. "We can't eat all these tomatoes before they go bad." Ella carefully spilled them from her apron onto the kitchen table. "And I've got plenty canned already. Put these with the stuff going to shantytown tonight. And those three eggs. We'll have fresh delivered in the morning, so I don't need them."

"Yes, ma'am."

Ella checked the fryers that had been stuffed with seasoned corn bread and placed in a shallow pan, ready for roasting. "Did you salt them?"

"And peppered one. Them old ladies don't like pepper, but Mr. Rainwater does."

Ella pushed back strands of hair that had escaped her bun. "Is Solly still with him?"

"In the back parlor doing they's lessons."

Ella opened the icebox. "One of us will need to go to the store tomorrow. Remind me to add a pound of butter to the grocery list."

"Mr. Rainwater sure is nice to be taking such notice of our Solly. Why do you reckon that is?"

"We need mayonnaise, too. And some bologna. If you're the one who goes, ask Mr. Randall to slice it more thinly this time, please."

"He sure be different."

Ella knew Margaret wasn't referring to the grocer. Closing the icebox door, she came around to face her maid. "Different?"

"Different from Mr. Barron."

Ella moved to the sink and washed her hands. "Mr. Rainwater has dark hair. He's lean. Mr. Barron was shorter, stockier, and had fair hair." She dried her hands and headed for the door. "I'm going to check on Solly, then I'll get that squash ready to bake."

"Wasn't talking about his looks."

Ella pretended not to hear her maid's mumbled parting remark and continued on to the parlor. Solly and Mr. Rainwater were seated in adjacent chairs at the card table where the Dunne sisters often played gin rummy.

When she walked in, Mr. Rainwater looked up at her and smiled. "I think you're wrong."

"About what?"

"I think Solly does grasp the concept of numbers. Watch."

She moved closer. A deck of playing cards had been scattered facedown over the table. The twos of each suit were neatly stacked, so were the threes and fours. As she watched, Solly picked all the fives from the scattered cards, starting with the club, then the spade, the heart, and the diamond last. He lined up the edges evenly and placed the group beside the stack of fours. He did the same with the sixes and sevens, choosing them unseen from the scattered deck, picking them out in the same sequence.

Ella wasn't all that encouraged. "He remembers where each card is on the table. It's a miracle, but he's not really learning. He's only matching the pattern of clubs on a card with the pattern of spades on another, and so on. What he's doing really has nothing to do with the quantities and how they relate."

"I'm not so sure. Cards, unlike dominoes, have the numbers printed on them."

"Does that make a difference?"

"I believe so. Keep watching."

Solly continued until he had stacked the tens besides the nines. Then he sat back and began to rock.

Ella looked at Mr. Rainwater, then at the cards still lying facedown on the table. "He didn't pick face cards or aces."

"They don't have numerals."

She sat down in the other chair, adjacent to Solly and across from Mr. Rainwater. Gathering all the stacks Solly had made, along with the cards still on the table, she shuffled the deck, then spread the cards out, first faceup, then turned them over one by one until all fifty-two were facedown.

Solly watched intently. As soon as all the cards were overturned, he actually pushed her hands aside so he could begin. He collected all the twos and proceeded until his stack of tens was placed neatly beside the stack of nines. He left the face cards and the aces.

Mr. Rainwater looked across at Ella, his eyebrow cocked. "He knows that the numerals represent the amount of symbols on each card, and he knows the sequence of the numbers. Four is greater than three."

Still doubtful, she murmured, "Possibly."

"He does."

"How do you know?"

"Because before you came in, I removed the fours from the deck. He stopped at three and didn't proceed until I'd returned the fours to the cards scattered on the table. I did it again with the eights. He stopped at seven, and that time, he reached into my coat pocket and took out the eights, arranged them in his sequence—clubs, spades, hearts, diamonds—and went from there."

Almost more miraculous to her than Solly's grasp of the numerals was that he'd voluntarily touched someone. "He reached into your pocket?"

Mr. Rainwater smiled. "With no guidance from me."

Her gaze shifted back to Solly. Reflexively, she stroked his cheek and said, "Good job, Solly." He batted her hand away, but she hoped that, in some inaccessible recess of his brain, her pride and love registered.

Looking back at the man across the table, she said, "Thank you for spending so much time with him."

"My pleasure."

"If he can learn to recognize numbers, if he learns their relevance to each other, he might be able to learn the same about letters. He could learn to do simple arithmetic, he could learn to read."

"That's my thinking."

"At least there's hope. There's always hope, right?"

His smile slipped, but only a fraction. "Not always. But sometimes."

The following morning Ella was in the dining room clearing the breakfast dishes when Margaret burst through the door of the kitchen. Her hat was askew, her face beaded with perspiration, and she was trying to catch her breath.

"What in the world?" Ella exclaimed.

Miss Violet was affronted. "Well, I never." She and her sister, frozen in motion, stared at the colored woman, aghast.

Mr. Rainwater surged to his feet. "What's wrong?"

"I heard it at the store," Margaret gasped. "There may be trouble out the Thompsons' place."

"Ollie and Lola's?" Ella asked.

"That's right. Your friends."

"I must go." Her heart in her throat, Ella gave her apron strings a yank, and when it came off, she handed it to Margaret as she squeezed in through the door connecting the dining room and kitchen.

She put on her hat, then knelt down and lifted Solly out of the chair where he sat tapping his cereal spoon against the edge of the table. "Finish up breakfast, Margaret. Put the groceries away. If I'm not back by lunchtime—"

"You go on, see to your friends," Margaret said. "I'll take care of things here, whether them old ladies like it or not."

"I'll drive you." This from Mr. Rainwater, who'd followed them into the kitchen.

"No, I'll take my car."

"Your car ain't been started since—"

"I can drive myself, Margaret," Ella snapped.

"But my car is parked out front."

Ella divided a look between her maid and her boarder, who'd extended the commonsense offer of taking his car, which was newer, more reliable, and easily accessible. "Thank you, Mr. Rainwater." She preceded him down the center hallway, carrying Solly, who was now tapping his spoon against her shoulder bone.

EIGHT

"They're your friends?"

Ella had tucked Solly between her and Mr. Rainwater in the front seat of his car. She'd given him directions out of town. He was driving fast, faster than she would have dared to push her older-model Ford.

"We went through school in the same class, although they dropped out in tenth grade. Ollie's daddy died, leaving him to take over the management of the dairy. He was the youngest child, and the only boy. All his sisters were married and long gone.

"There was never any doubt that he and Lola would get married someday. They'd always been crazy about each other. When Ollie left school, Lola insisted they go ahead and make it official, so she could help out on the farm, too. They've got four children now. They're good people. Take a right at the next crossroads."

The road onto which Mr. Rainwater turned was unpaved. Tall weeds grew in the ditches on both sides. Beyond the ditches, barbed-wire fences separated rows of corn plants struggling for survival in the arid soil from fields of cotton being picked by workers trailing long sacks on their bowed backs.

It wasn't yet ten o'clock, but Ella guessed that already the temperature was topping ninety. They had no choice except to leave the car windows down. The wind was hot and gritty. It had whipped off Ella's hat and was tearing at her hair, but she barely noticed.

Her thoughts were on her friends and their misfortune. With each baby, Lola had grown a little chubbier, and the gap between her front teeth seemed to widen, but she was one of the happiest individuals Ella had ever known. She loved her husband, loved her children, loved her life. Ella hoped her innate happiness would sustain her and her family through this.

Ollie was a salt-of-the-earth type, big-eared and bighearted. He'd struggled to pass from one school grade to the next because of all the days he had to miss in order to help his father work their farm, milking the herd before and after school and doing everything else required to maintain the place. But Ollie had given up school willingly. Know-how had been more valuable to him than book learning, and his hands-on experience had paid off. He took pride in how much the farm had prospered under his supervision.

At least until the past few years, when he'd been forced to borrow money to sustain his herd and his family until the drought ended and his grazing pastures turned green again. What milk he could get from his underfed cows, he'd had to sell cheap, creating a need for another loan. That vicious cycle had put him and Lola deeply in debt and in danger of losing their farm.

They would benefit greatly from the DRS's program to buy their herd for pennies on the dollar, but at what cost emotionally?

Mr. Rainwater said, "I'm afraid we're too late."

Ella spotted the cloud of dust rising out of the roadbed almost at the same time he spoke. "What is it?"

"A convoy, I suspect."

The distance between them and the column of swirling dust closed rapidly. They were almost even with it before they could pick out individual vehicles. In the lead was a cattle truck with dairy cows crammed inside. Following it were three black cars, all with insignias painted on the sides, dour-faced men inside. One man in the first car was standing on the running board, holding on to an open window, a rifle propped on his shoulder.

"Are they the—"

"Shooters," Mr. Rainwater said, finishing for her.

Over the roar of the passing cars, she heard another sound, which at first she thought was one of the cars backfiring. But when Mr. Rainwater said a swearword under his breath, she noticed how tightly he was gripping the steering wheel, how tensely his jaw was set.

"What's that popping noise?"

"Gunfire."

She turned her head and watched as the government cars disappeared behind a swell in the road. The gunshots weren't coming from them. So who was shooting? A cold knot of fear formed in her chest. To help stave it off, she said, "This is different from what happened at the Pritchetts' place."

Mr. Rainwater turned his head and gave her a significant look.

Protesting her own misgivings, she said, "That happened because of the folks in shantytown. But none of them would come out this far. They wouldn't have any way to get here. So who's shooting? And why?"

She was still disturbed by images of the injuries she had seen inflicted on women and children. She remembered Brother Calvin's account of the toddler being snatched from Mrs. Pritchett's arms while Sheriff Anderson and his deputies did nothing. Suddenly she was very afraid for her friends.

"Hurry," she urged, leaning forward as though willing the car to go faster. "It's the next left."

Just before they reached the turnoff to the Thompsons' farm, a pickup spun out onto the road, made a sharp right turn, and headed straight toward them. The truck fishtailed in the loose gravel, almost throwing several men out of its bed before it straightened. It stayed in their lane until the very last moment, then, with a blast of the horn, it swerved to cross the yellow stripe.

The truck buffeted Mr. Rainwater's coupe as it zoomed past. Ella recognized the man at the wheel—Conrad Ellis. Crowded into the cab with him were three other men. There were a dozen or so in the truck bed, hanging on to each other and whatever else they could for stability. None seemed too concerned about the possibility of being pitched out. They were laughing, whooping, firing pistols and deer rifles into the air.

Mr. Rainwater took the left turn practically on two wheels, throwing Solly against Ella and Ella against the passenger door. It was a quarter mile between the main road and the farmhouse. Mr. Rainwater kept the accelerator on the floorboard until they were even with a pasture where a large pit had been dug. He braked suddenly. The car skidded several yards before it came to a stop.

Mr. Rainwater got out and walked around the hood of the

car. He removed his hat and tapped it against his thigh as he surveyed the mass grave. Solly seemed content to be tapping the toes of his shoes together, so Ella got out, too.

When Brother Calvin had recounted the incident at the Pritchetts' farm, he'd painted vivid word pictures to describe the scene. But the preacher's graphic depiction hadn't adequately prepared Ella for what she saw. Several dozen scrawny cows and calves had been herded into the pit and shot through their heads, some several times. They'd fallen one on top of the other, legs tangled. It was a sickening sight.

"This is the damnedest thing."

She realized that Mr. Rainwater was speaking mostly to himself, and, anyway, what could she possibly add? Shading her eyes against the glaring sun, she looked toward the grove of willow trees where two tractors with front loaders were parked. The men operating them were waiting in the shade before finishing their job of burial. One was smoking a cigarette. The other had pulled his hat low over his face, apparently dozing.

Ella had to remind herself that they, and the marksmen, too, were men doing the best they could to earn a living in the throes of a terrible economy. They hadn't conceived the policy they were being paid to implement, and possibly understood it even less than she. They were just men, doing a tough job during tough times.

Nevertheless, she felt as though they were the enemy.

Turning away, she checked on Solly, who was still fixated on tapping his shoes together, then started walking up the incline toward the house. The sun felt blazing hot on the top of her head, reminding her that she'd left her hat on the seat of the car. But she didn't go back for it.

A white picket fence enclosed the yard in front of the

house. The house was also white, but it was now pockmarked here and there with black dots. Ella realized with shock that these were fresh bullet holes. When she reached the fence, she saw that the gate had been torn off the post and left to lie in a red ant bed. The ants were in an angry frenzy. Ella carefully stepped over what was left of the anthill.

Lola was sitting in the porch swing, her hands to her face, crying into her apron. Two solemn-faced children sat, one on either side of her. The boy, obviously the older, was dry-eyed but much too young for the embittered expression on his smooth face.

The little girl was resting one hand on her mother's knee. Tear tracks were on her cheeks. She stopped crying as she watched Ella cross the yard and climb the steps onto the porch.

"Ollie."

He was sitting on the top step, his beefy shoulders hunched, his work boots planted on the step below. A cigarette hung between his lips. Almost an inch of ash dangled from it. He was holding a Colt pistol in his right hand, but his grip was so loose, the gun seemed on the verge of slipping from his grasp. He was staring into near space, seemingly unaware of Ella's approach, but when she spoke his name, he looked up at her with haunted eyes.

"Ella." Coming to himself, he removed the cigarette from his mouth and reached beneath the step to grind it out, asking, "What are you doing out here?"

"I came . . . I thought you might be upset. I came to lend whatever support I can."

His gaze shifted to the car parked in the lane, still a distance from the house. He spotted Mr. Rainwater where he stood staring forlornly at the crater in the pasture. "Who's that?"

Mr. Rainwater couldn't have heard them from that distance, but just as Ollie asked about him, he turned away from the gruesome sight and started walking toward the house.

"A distant cousin of Dr. Kincaid's. He's staying in town for a while. He's boarding with me."

They watched Mr. Rainwater as he walked up the lane and through the damaged gate. As he entered the yard, Ella was struck by how thin he was compared to Ollie.

"Mr. Thompson?" he said as he approached. "David Rainwater."

Ollie stared at the right hand extended to him as though unsure what to do with it. Then he shifted the revolver to his left hand and shook hands. "Ollie Thompson."

"I hate that we're meeting under these circumstances."

"Yeah, me, too." With an effort, Ollie pulled himself up. Even when he was standing, it looked as though his shoulders were bearing a tremendous weight.

"We saw the cattle truck. Did they pay you fairly?" Mr. Rainwater asked.

"Going rate. Sixteen a head, plus a three-dollar bonus on each. Even for the calves. I'm glad to get it. I applied for the relief. But, hell, it was awful."

Ella left the men to their solemn conversation and moved to the swing. Lola blotted her eyes and, looking up at Ella, gave her a weak version of her gap-toothed smile. She patted her son on the back. "Scoot," she said to him. "Let Mrs. Barron sit down."

The boy left the swing and jumped off the porch. Hands forced deep into the pockets of his overalls, he disappeared around the corner of the house.

"He's upset," Lola said as Ella sat down in the swing beside her. "I hope he'll get over it." Looking at Ollie, she added in an undertone, "I hope his daddy will."

Ella smiled at the little girl, who gave her a shy smile back, then rested her head against Lola's plump arm. "Where are your other children?"

"I called my mama this morning and told her to come get them and keep them until the cows are buried. These two are having a hard enough time with it. I didn't want the younger two scarred for life by seeing something they can't understand."

"What happened?"

Tears welled up in the woman's eyes. "The men with the tractors got here just after daylight and dug the hole. Then the men in the government cars arrived and sorted the herd. Loaded the healthier ones onto the truck. The rest . . ." She nodded toward the pit.

"Forty head," Ollie said. There were tears standing in his eyes now. "I took money for them. I had no choice," he said, his voice cracking. "I gotta make a loan payment or lose this place. This is my daddy's place. I had to save it."

He was unable to go on, so Lola continued for him. "Soon's the government men got them into the pit, they started shootin'. Those poor mama cows and their babies." She began crying in earnest. Ella placed an arm across her shoulders.

"What about the truckload of rabble-rousers?"

"We saw Conrad on the road," Ella said, clarifying Mr. Rainwater's question.

Ollie hawked up a wad of phlegm and spat it into the dirt off the edge of the porch. "White trash son'bitch."

"Ollie," Lola said, nodding toward their daughter.

"Well, he is. For all the money he and his daddy have, they're trash. That whole branch of Ellises is rotten to the core. Ever' damn last one of 'em."

"What were they doing here?" Mr. Rainwater asked.

"What I think is, those government cowards brung them along just in case." Ollie spat again.

"In case of what?" Mr. Rainwater asked.

"I tried bargaining with the head guy," Ollie said angrily. "Told him he didn't have to turn his shooters loose, that I'd get rid of those cows myself. Told him I'd take the best of the lot to shantytown. Let those folks have at 'em and get at least one good meal for their kids.

"But no. He said he had orders to shoot and bury those that were culled and that's what he was going to do, and I couldn't stop him. Fine, I said. You go ahead and be the government's whore." He wiped tears from his eyes. "'Course I'm a whore, too, I reckon, for taking his goddamn check."

"Hush that talk right now, Ollie Thompson! You did what you had to."

He looked at his wife remorsefully. "Don't make it right, Lola. It don't make me feel good about it." He paused for a moment before continuing. "I guess the man didn't take me at my word, because while they were shooting the cows, Conrad and his bunch had their guns trained on us, like we was going to try and stop them. When it was over, the government men left. But before Conrad peeled out, he and his cronies shot up my house."

Mr. Rainwater's eyes picked out several splintered bullet holes in the wood. "Why?"

"Meanness, I guess." Ollie ran his sleeve under his nose. "Or else to scare me into doing nothin', which is what I did."

He glanced in the direction of where his son had rounded the corner of the house. "Made my boy ashamed of me, I think."

"What could you have done, Ollie?" Lola asked, her staunch loyalty showing. "Picked a fight with Conrad and got us all shot?"

"She's right," Mr. Rainwater said. "Based on what I've heard of this Ellis character, it would have been foolhardy to provoke him."

Ella told them what had happened when Mr. Pritchett tried to face him down. "We had an eyewitness tell us how he grabbed the child right out of Mrs. Pritchett's arms."

"If he'd laid a hand on Lola or one of my kids, I'd've killed him," Ollie said.

Lola must have noticed Ella looking at the pistol in Ollie's hand. Nervously she scoffed. "He wouldn't really shoot somebody."

"Hell I wouldn't," the man declared. "Swear to God I would've."

Speaking to Mr. Rainwater, Lola said, "One of the calves that was shot didn't die right away. Conrad and his friends heard it bawling. They stood at the rim of the pit, laughing and chucking rocks down at it."

"Like I said," Ollie muttered. "Trash."

"Ollie went inside the house to get his pistol and put the poor thing outta its misery. But those boys wouldn't let Ollie go near that pit. Finally the calf died, I guess. He stopped bawling. Conrad and his friends piled into that pickup of his and left."

"Party over."

Ella noticed that whenever Mr. Rainwater was extremely angry, his lips barely moved when he spoke. He caught her looking at him now. She quickly averted her gaze to Ollie.

He said, "Them cows would have died soon anyway. I had

no way to feed them. They were starving." He swallowed. "But, let me tell you, seeing them just shot like that was something terrible to behold."

He raised his chin toward the grove where the two men with the tractors were climbing back onto the seats of their machines. "All that's left to do is spray on lye and shove dirt back into the hole."

As they watched, the tractor motors were cranked to life. Making a racket and belching exhaust, the tractors started chugging toward the mass grave.

Ella laid her hand on Lola's arm. "Is there anything I can do for you?"

She raised her apron to her eyes to blot them and, to everyone's surprise, began chuckling. Lowering the apron, she said, "You can get on your knees and thank the good Lord that Ollie didn't shoot Conrad Ellis right between the eyes."

Ella appreciated the other woman's resilience and irrepressible humor. If Ella had experienced what Lola had that morning, she didn't believe she could even attempt a laugh.

"I'm glad Ollie didn't have to shoot that calf, either," Lola added. "Butchering an animal for food is one thing. Killing one for any other reason, well, that's somethin' else. He had to put down an old horse once, and he cried hisself to sleep three nights in a row on account of it."

She spoke with an affection produced by long-standing love for Ollie Thompson. The look the two exchanged was so personal, and spoke such volumes about how they felt about each other, that Ella felt like an intruder on an intensely private moment. She also felt a pang of envy.

The swing rocked gently as she stood up. "I ran out on Margaret, so I'd better get back to the house."

"Thank you for coming," Lola said.

"I didn't do anything."

"Just coming was something." Lola looked at Mr. Rainwater. "I ain't actually made your acquaintance. I'm Lola. Thank you for driving Ella out here."

"You're welcome, Mrs. Thompson. I wish better times for you."

Lola pulled her daughter close and kissed the top of her head. "Any better and I'd be spoiled, Mr. Rainwater."

Obviously liking her and her optimistic outlook, he smiled.

Then they all heard it at the same time—a calf's bawl coming from the pit.

"Oh, Lord, have mercy," Lola moaned.

The little girl began to cry.

The boy, who'd run away, reappeared. This time his eyes were wet. He looked at the adults on the porch with renewed horror.

Ollie closed his eyes briefly, then started down the steps.

Mr. Rainwater reached out and grabbed his arm. "No. I'll take care of it." He didn't wait for Ollie to either protest or concede, nor did he take the pistol but strode across the yard and through the gap in the fence, his long legs covering ground quickly.

The bawling became more frantic, a horrible sound. Ella gave Lola a quick hug and patted Ollie's arm as she rushed past him, calling back, "Let me know if you need anything." Then she rushed down the steps and through the gate.

By the time she reached the pit, Mr. Rainwater was going over the edge of it. The slope wasn't all that steep, but the earth was loose and he was wearing dress shoes, not work boots like Ollie's. He almost lost his footing several times on his descent into the mass grave. The tractors were almost upon it.

Ella watched helplessly as Mr. Rainwater awkwardly made his way toward the calf, whose hindquarters were trapped beneath a carcass, presumably that of its mother. The animal had a wound on its back that was bloody and already flyblown, but obviously not fatal.

One of the tractor drivers shouted, "Hey! What the hell? Get outta there!"

Mr. Rainwater ignored him and continued trying to find the best path through the carcasses to the injured calf.

"Crazy damn fool!" the other tractor driver yelled.

"I'm warning you, mister!" shouted the first.

Either Mr. Rainwater didn't hear them or he was deliberately paying no attention to their implied threats. The calf continued to bawl. Mr. Rainwater picked up a boulder the size of a watermelon, then carried it, with apparent difficulty, over to the calf. He raised the stone high above his head, then dropped it onto the animal's head, crushing its skull, killing it instantly, silencing the plaintive bawling.

Ella covered her mouth and pressed her arm across her middle.

Mr. Rainwater bent at the waist and placed his hands on his knees. He remained like that for several moments, until one of the tractor drivers shouted another curse at him and threatened him with a face full of lye.

Only then did he straighten up and, with an effort, begin climbing the incline of loose earth.

Ella, shaken by what she'd witnessed, turned toward the car. She drew up short, gasping hot air into her lungs, startled to see Solly standing beside the car, his stare fixed on the carcasses in the pit and the man climbing out of it.

NINE

Little was said on the drive back into town. Ella didn't know where Mr. Rainwater's thoughts were, but hers were on Solly. She worried about how much he'd seen, how much of it he'd comprehended, and what effect such a grisly sight might have on him. As soon as she'd ushered him back into the car, he had resumed tapping the toes of his shoes together. He seemed unaffected, but there was no way of knowing for certain what kind of impact the incident had made.

As for her, it had left deep impressions: the pit of bony carcasses, Lola and Ollie in such despair, the sound of the calf's desperate bawling, and the sudden silence after Mr. Rainwater killed it. She feared it would be a long time before those disturbing memories receded.

They plagued her as she slogged through her chores that afternoon. The heat was blistering and enervating, so that even the most routine task seemed insurmountable. The Dunne sisters pulled her aside and complained of Margaret's uppity attitude. Ella promised to speak to the maid about it, and when she did, Margaret reacted with a sudden recoil that caused her to splash grease out of the large iron skillet in which she was frying salmon croquettes. The grease landed in the gas flame, which started a small fire on the stove and filled the kitchen with fishy-smelling smoke.

By late afternoon, Ella's stamina and patience were spent. She wanted only to get through the dinner hour and the cleanup, then retreat with Solly to their rooms, where she hoped she could find some peace and quiet.

With that in mind, Ella set the dining room table while Margaret was shredding cabbage for slaw and mixing a corn bread batter. When Ella returned to the kitchen, she discovered Mr. Rainwater sitting at the table with Solly, who was lining up rows of toothpicks on the floral-patterned oilcloth.

Mr. Rainwater smiled up at her. "He's making real progress. He's forming groups of ten after watching me do it only once. And each time he reaches into the box for the toothpicks, he takes out an even ten."

Ella took a pitcher of tea from the icebox and placed it on a serving tray. "That's not progress, Mr. Rainwater. That's a worthless trick."

Margaret stopped stirring the batter and gave Ella a disapproving glance over her shoulder, which Ella pretended not to see.

Several moments of tense silence elapsed, then Mr. Rainwater asked quietly, "Why do you say that?"

Keeping her back to him, Ella added a sugar bowl and a dish of freshly sliced lemons to the tray. "You heard what Dr. Kincaid said. Solly's talent, for lack of a better word, has no practical application. Not unless somebody needs their toothpicks lined up in rows of ten, or their dominoes arranged in a row in ascending order."

"I'm stunned to hear you say that."

She came around to him quickly. "Why?"

"Because this could be a breakthrough. A start. The initial step toward—"

"What, Mr. Rainwater?" She motioned down at Solly, who was placing the toothpicks equidistantly apart while tapping his heels against the legs of his chair. "What is this moving him toward? A parlor act? Something to entertain the socialites in Dallas or Houston?"

In a carnival barker's voice, she said, "Come and see Solomon Barron. He screeches like a banshee and flaps his hands and throws tantrums every time his mother touches him, but he's a whiz at card tricks."

"Miss Ella?" Margaret had turned away from the counter. Thick, yellow batter was dripping onto the floor off the wooden spoon she held in her hand, but she was so dismayed over Ella's emotional unraveling that she failed to notice. "What's come over you?"

"Nothing. Nothing!" Ella said, her voice cracking. "I'm just trying to explain to Mr. Rainwater, who, for reasons unknown, has taken on my son as a pet project, how ridiculous and futile his lessons are."

She took a step toward the table. "I don't want my son to be a freak, on exhibit for people's amusement. I don't want him to be a sideshow. I want him to read and write and *talk* to me, not . . . not . . . ." Furiously she raked her hand across the table, sending Solly's carefully arranged rows of toothpicks and the open box of them to the linoleum.

Solly immediately emitted an ear-piercing shriek and began striking the sides of his head with his fists.

Ella, suddenly silenced and immobilized by her behavior, gaped at the toothpicks scattered across the floor, disbelieving what she'd done. She wouldn't have thought herself capable of losing control so quickly and completely.

Mr. Rainwater calmly stood and went for the broom to sweep up the toothpicks. Margaret returned the dripping spoon to the bowl of batter, saying softly to Ella, "See to the boy, Miss Ella. I'll take care of this."

Ella, mortified by her outburst, nodded and pulled Solly from his chair. It was a struggle, but she finally got him, kicking and screaming, into his room. She closed the door so that only she had to withstand his tantrum.

It was violent and went on for almost half an hour. Nothing she did subdued him. She dodged his fists and feet as best she could but knew that tomorrow she would have bruises. Eventually he exhausted himself enough to fall asleep.

Ella sat on his bed and wept copiously.

The frustration and sorrow that had been building inside her all day erupted in great, gulping sobs. She cried over her friends Ollie and Lola, who could now stave off foreclosure but only by paying a tremendous emotional price. She cried over their children who'd experienced such a horrible thing beyond their understanding. And over the Dunne sisters, who were reduced to living in someone else's house and occupying themselves by complaining about the help. And over Margaret, who had to endure their prejudice.

And in a rare moment of self-pity, she cried over herself and Solly and their plight.

She lived in fear of their future. Daily she strove to keep her fears at bay and not let them govern her. But today she didn't have the strength to ward them off, and they assailed her.

When Solly grew larger and stronger than she, how would she control his tantrums?

What would happen to him if something happened to her? Adults in their prime contracted terminal illnesses. Like Mr. Rainwater. What if she got a cancer and died? Where would Solly be sent to live out the rest of his days?

People also had fatal accidents. They got hit by cars, struck by lightning, impaled on pitchforks. People died silly, stupid, senseless deaths doing a household chore they'd done a thousand times without mishap. If she died unexpectedly, what would become of Solly?

Or what if he injured someone during one of his tantrums? He would be taken from her and placed in an asylum, and people would say that was better for everyone. Everyone except Solly.

Eventually she cried herself out. Then, ashamed of her tears, she washed her face with cold water until her eyes were a little less puffy and red. She tidied her hair and replaced her apron with a fresh one. She checked Solly one more time, then left her room.

The house was quiet. Dinner was over and the dining room had been cleared. Margaret was finishing up the dishes in the kitchen. "I saved you a plate, Miss Ella." It was in the center of the table, covered with a cloth.

"Thank you, Margaret," she said, but she made no move toward the table.

The woman looked at her with concern. "You want something else? I'll stay, fix you anything you like."

Ella shook her head. "I'm not very hungry. You go on." Seeing Margaret's hesitation, she added, "My crying jag is over. Solly's sleeping. We're fine. I'll see you in the morning."

Margaret removed her apron and put on her hat, then crossed to Ella and gave her a hug. "Today's troubles is past now. Tomorrow will be better."

That turned out not to be true.

Mr. Rainwater didn't come down for breakfast. Ella figured he was disinclined to leave his room out of pique over her harsh words to him yesterday afternoon. Unfairly she had unleashed her frustration on him, although he was responsible for some of it. She had meant every word she'd said about not wanting Solly to become an object of curiosity and morbid fascination, like England's Elephant Man.

But in her heart of hearts, she knew that wasn't Mr. Rainwater's intention. Not at all. His wanting to plumb the depths of Solly's abilities was honorable and kind. She had no reason to think he wanted to exploit Solly, certainly not for self-gain.

She planned to apologize for her rudeness, but the morning passed without his coming downstairs. She didn't become concerned until he failed to appear at lunch. Margaret confirmed that she hadn't seen him all day. Neither had the Dunne sisters.

"Nothing's wrong, I hope," Miss Violet said tremulously.

"He's probably just trying to evade the heat."

But Ella doubted her own explanation and decided to check on him. Leaving Solly in Margaret's care, she went upstairs. As she walked down the long hallway, she made certain her footfalls could be heard, not wanting him to think she was sneaking up on him to spy.

She paused outside his door and listened but heard no sounds coming from the other side. "Mr. Rainwater?" She tapped lightly on the door, then pressed her fist against her lips, waiting for a reply. None came. She knocked softly again. "Mr. Rainwater, are you all right?"

When he didn't answer, her mouth went dry. Her heart began to thud dully with apprehension. Dr. Kincaid had said six to twelve weeks. Possibly more if he was fortunate. He said Mr. Rainwater would have good days and bad, but the steady decline as the cancer spread was inevitable. There would be pain. Eventually the systems of his body would begin shutting down one by one, but the doctor had promised to have him taken to a hospital well before then.

"I won't let him die in your house, Mrs. Barron. You'll have plenty of warning before it comes to that. God would be merciful to take him quickly, but it rarely happens that swiftly."

But now she wondered if Dr. Kincaid had been wrong about the course the illness would take, wrong about God and His mercy.

With her heart in her throat, she opened the door to his room.

He was lying on the bed outside the covers, dressed in shirt, pants, and socks, but by the look of the twisted bedding beneath him, he'd been there for a while. He'd placed one forearm over his eyes; the other hand was clutching the cloth of his shirt above his stomach. She was vastly relieved to see that he was breathing, although his respiration was light and fast and made a soughing sound as it passed through his partially opened lips. The sour smell of sweat permeated the room.

"Mr. Rainwater?"

He made a feeble motion with the arm resting over his eyes. "Please go, Mrs. Barron."

Instead, she approached the bed. "Do you need me to call Dr. Kincaid?"

"I—" Before he could finish, he was gripped by what appeared to be an excruciating pain. He strained a groan through gritted teeth.

Ella spun around and ran from the room, shouting for Margaret as she raced down the hallway. By the time she had clattered down the stairs, Margaret was standing at the bottom of them, her eyes wide with alarm. "Is somethin' the matter with Mr. Rainwater?"

"He's sick. Call Dr. Kincaid. Tell him to come immediately."

Ella actually gave Margaret a push toward the telephone as she brushed past her. She went into the formal parlor and unplugged the fan. On her way back to the staircase, she spotted the Dunne sisters standing together in the archway of the informal parlor, holding hands, looking both concerned and fearful. "Is there anything we can do?" asked Miss Pearl.

"No, but thank you."

Ella could hear Margaret speaking to the telephone operator. Quickly she went back upstairs, taking the fan with her.

Mr. Rainwater was as she'd left him, but the spasm that had seized him seemed to have abated. He lowered his arm from his eyes when she came in. "Please, Mrs. Barron, don't fret. Bad spells like this are to be expected. I'll get through it."

"In the meantime, this should make you more comfortable." She set the fan on the table in front of the window and plugged it in. "How long have you been suffering like this?"

"Since last night."

"Last night! Why didn't you let me know so I could call Dr. Kincaid?"

"I thought it would pass. I'm sure it will."

She didn't share his optimism. His lips were rimmed white with agony, and his fist still had a damp grip on the cloth of his shirt. His eyes were sunk deeply into their sockets. "Dr. Kincaid will be here shortly. Do you want me to get you something to drink? Tea?"

He gave his head a small shake. "Water, maybe."

She hesitated, then left him again, making her way hastily to the kitchen. The elderly sisters had disappeared, presumably back into the informal parlor. Margaret looked at her expectantly when she barged through the kitchen door.

"Is it the summer fever, Miss Ella?"

"I suppose, yes. Is Dr. Kincaid coming?"

"Right away, he said."

"Good. Get the water pitcher from the icebox. And a drinking glass. Where's that porcelain basin we wash vegetables in?"

"Same place it's always at."

Ella found the basin on its customary shelf in the pantry. She put it, the pitcher of cooled water, and the glass on a tray. "Stay with Solly." He was sitting on the floor underneath the table, playing with empty spools. Ella put her back to the door and pushed it open. "Send the doctor up the moment he arrives."

Upstairs in Mr. Rainwater's room, she moved aside a book, his watch, and the small reading lamp in order to place the tray on his nightstand. She poured water from the pitcher into the glass, then slid her hand beneath his head and lifted it. He drank thirstily and signaled her when he'd had enough. She returned his head to the pillow, noting that it was soggy with perspiration.

"I'll be right back."

She left again, taking the basin with her. She half filled it with cold water from the bathroom faucet and took a clean washcloth from the cabinet. Being careful not to slosh the water out of the basin, she returned it to the nightstand and dipped the cloth in it. She wrung it out and used it to bathe his face. He watched her for a moment, then closed his eyes. "Thank you."

"You're welcome."

"Did you tend your husband?"

"Pardon?"

"I assumed Mr. Barron died of an illness. Did you tend to him? Is that how you acquired your nurse's touch?"

"He died suddenly."

"Oh." After a moment, he added, "Then your nursing skills come to you naturally."

She dipped the cloth in the water again, wrung it out, applied it to his face and neck. "I think it's part of the maternal instinct."

Although his eyes remained closed, he smiled faintly. "A feminine skill, unique to your sex."

She wet the cloth again and, after wringing it out, folded it into a rectangle and laid it on his forehead, pressing it into place. Then she withdrew and sat down in the chair near the window, clasping her hands in her lap. He said nothing more, and she would have thought that he was asleep except for the occasional contraction of his fingers and the tightening of his jaw, indications that he was experiencing gripping pains.

Through the open window she heard the arrival of Dr. Kincaid's car, the closing of the car door, his hurried footsteps up the walkway and onto the porch. Moments later, he appeared in the open doorway, looking out of breath and anxious. "David?" With barely a glance toward Ella, he moved to the bed, set his black medical bag on the foot of it, and bent over his patient with obvious concern.

Mr. Rainwater opened his eyes. "Hello, Murdy. Don't look so scared. I'm still alive."

Ella stood. "I'll leave you. If you need anything . . ."

"Of course, Mrs. Barron. Thank you," the doctor said absently.

She went out, pulling the door closed behind her.

TEN

It was almost half an hour before Dr. Kincaid came downstairs. The Dunne sisters had gone to visit a friend. Margaret was cooking dinner while keeping an eye on Solly. The doctor found Ella in the informal parlor, where she was using a dust mop on the hardwood floor.

"How is he?"

Dr. Kincaid removed a handkerchief from his pants pocket and wiped his face and bald head. Ella wondered if this habit was merely to blot up perspiration, or if he used it to delay imparting bad news. "I gave him something. The crisis is past."

"He was in terrible pain."

"The worst he's experienced so far."

His inflection implied that today's pain was only a harbinger of what was to come.

"I've left him something to give himself. He says he won't

use it unless the pain becomes unbearable. He's stubborn on that point. For now," he added grimly. "He'll change his mind."

Ella looked away. After a moment, she asked, "Isn't there anything that could be done? Surgery? A treatment of some kind?"

"If there was, he'd already have had it, Mrs. Barron. I would have seen to it."

"Of course. I didn't mean to imply any negligence on your part."

"I know you didn't, and I didn't take it that way. Believe me, I share your frustration. I've researched every outlet I know of. I've written to doctors who have a lot more experience and knowledge. Specialists as far away as Boston and New York. They all arrive at the same sad prognosis. It started in his bones and went undetected until it metastasized to vital organs."

Ella brushed a stray curl off her forehead. "Do you have any instructions for me?"

"He's not your patient."

"But he lives under my roof. I can't simply ignore him if he's in agony."

"Call me at the first sign of discomfort. Any time of the day or night, don't hesitate to send for me, no matter how loudly David protests."

"I will."

"He'll always say it isn't necessary."

"His objections will fall on deaf ears."

"Good."

She walked the doctor to the front door and unlatched the screen. He hesitated on the threshold and looked at her remorsefully. "You didn't need this additional strain, Mrs. Barron. I shouldn't have brought David to you. I regret now that I did."

The doctor's house was overcrowded with his two active, noisy sons. His patients called on him at all hours of the night. Coming into the clinic on a daily basis was a constant stream of people with bleeding wounds and broken bones, women in labor, children with ailments ranging from minor sore throats to life-threatening illnesses. She believed he'd brought Mr. Rainwater to her not to shirk his responsibility but so Mr. Rainwater would have a more peaceful place in which to live.

Hoping to alleviate his guilt, she told him that Mr. Rainwater was an ideal boarder. "He's considerate and well liked by the others. He's exceptionally patient with Solly. Even helpful." She was about to expound on that, but changed her mind. "Mr. Rainwater goes out of his way not to be a burden."

"I hope he doesn't become one to you." The doctor put on his hat and started down the steps, then halted and turned back. "On the other hand, Mrs. Barron, I wouldn't trust anyone else to take such good care of him."

She tapped on his door. "May I come in?"

"Please."

He was seated in the chair at the window. Through it, he watched the doctor drive away. "What did Murdy tell you?"

"He suggested I come up and change your bedding."

He turned his head and saw that she was carrying fresh, folded bedsheets. "I doubt that's what you two talked about."

"I noticed you could use fresh linens."

"Do they smell that bad? Murdy helped me wash and change into a clean shirt, but I should have known my sickbed wouldn't comply with your standards."

She was about to smile at the gentle gibe when she spotted the wicked-looking syringe. It was lying on the top of the bureau alongside a small black leather pouch, which she assumed contained vials of medication.

He followed her gaze. "Murdy's trying to turn me into a dope fiend."

"He doesn't want you to suffer needlessly."

He looked at the syringe with distaste, then turned his head away to look out the window again. Taking that as her cue to drop the subject, Ella moved to the bed and began stripping off the damp, wrinkled sheets.

"I would offer to help, but Murdy's pain reliever has left me feeling a little woozy."

"I'll be quick and then you can return to bed."

"Take your time. I spent all night and all day in bed. I'm not anxious to return to it. I enjoy the view from here." After a moment, he said, "I've been looking at the cottonwood tree across the street. When I was a boy, I climbed one that was as tall. One day, I was about a third of the way up when I came across a raccoon that was foaming at the mouth. I had to drop to the ground or get bit. I broke my arm."

"Better than getting rabies."

He gave a soft laugh. "It wasn't quick thinking on my part. The thing was hissing, scared the daylights out of me. My folks commended me for exercising good judgment by jumping, when in truth, I was so frightened I actually fell out of the tree. It's a wonder I didn't break my neck."

She smiled across at him. "Did you ever climb that tree again?"

"Soon as my arm was healed. I had to in order to restore my pride."

Turning back to the bed, she spread the bottom sheet over the mattress, then went around the bed, pulling the sheet tightly and tucking it in. "Mr. Rainwater?"

"Hmm?"

"I must apologize to you. For yesterday." She could feel his gaze on her back as she picked up the folded top sheet, unfurled it, let it settle over the bed. "The incident with the toothpicks. The things I said to you. I didn't mean them. It's not like me to fly off the handle like that. I don't know what came over me."

"You were upset about what happened to your friends."

She finished tucking the sheet into the foot of the bed, then straightened up and turned to face him. "Yes. But it wasn't only that." She bowed her head briefly, then raised it to look directly at him. "I was jealous."

"Jealous?"

"Of the progress you're making with Solly. And despite what I said yesterday, it *is* progress." Feeling the heat in her cheeks and knowing it must show, she turned her back to him again and picked up a pillow. Holding it between chin and chest, she pulled on the pillowcase, then placed the pillow precisely in the center of the headboard. "I don't know how far it will go, but your progress with him underscores my failure to reach him on any level."

She smoothed the bedspread over the bed, then folded it and the top sheet back at a perfect ninety-degree angle. After making one last adjustment to the counterpane, she turned. Astonishingly, he was standing directly in front of her. He was still in stocking feet, so she hadn't known he'd left the chair and moved up behind her, until now that they were face-to-face. And close.

"You have no reason to feel jealous. If I've made what you

perceive to be progress with Solly, it's because I have idle time to devote to him. You don't. You're too busy doing what you must to provide for him." He paused for a beat, then added, "At tremendous sacrifice to yourself."

That was a presumptuous statement. She could have taken issue with it, but she was afraid to have him expand upon what aspects of life he thought she was sacrificing. It seemed like a dangerous conversation to enter into, especially with him, especially in this room at this moment.

She had to swallow before she could speak. "It's very generous of you to think so."

"I'm not being generous. I'm stating the way things are."

Averting her head, she asked, "Do you accept my apology?"

"Even though it's unnecessary, yes."

"Thank you."

She stepped past him and was about to bend down to pick up the dirty sheets from the floor when he shocked her further by reaching for her hand. She was so startled by the unexpected contact that she looked at their hands to confirm it. And then she continued looking at them for a long time, noting the difference in size, in the texture of skin, in the pressure his fingers applied to hers. Finally she tilted her head up and looked into his face.

He said, "I hate that you saw me like that today."

"You were in pain."

"You were very calm."

"I only appeared to be."

"You bathed my face."

"It was the least I could do."

"It helped."

"I'm glad."

"Thank you."

"You're welcome."

For several seconds more, they remained connected by their hands and stares, then she pulled her hand from his and hastily gathered up the sheets. At the door, she said, "I'll have Margaret bring up your dinner on a tray."

"I'll be down for dinner."

"You should rest, Mr. Rainwater."

"I'll be down."

He was.

He seemed to suffer no lasting ill effects from the bad spell. Whether or not he was injecting the painkiller—Ella presumed it was morphine—she didn't know. But he definitely took a turn for the better. The very next day, he resumed working with Solly, but only after he had cleared it with her first.

"I don't want you flying off the handle again."

She didn't take umbrage because he said it with a teasing smile.

"I promise not to sling any more toothpicks. You can work with Solly any time you like."

He set aside time each day.

And, he began going out often. If he bothered to inform her at all that he was leaving the house, he would tell her only the approximate time he would be back. He never said where he was going. He didn't skip meals, so he wasn't eating out. If he drove to Waco to catch a movie, he never mentioned the films he saw.

Sometimes he was gone for only a short while in the afternoons. Other times, he left after dinner and didn't return until hours later. Of course, it was none of her business where he went, but she was curious—which she acknowledged only to herself.

"What do you figure is going on?" Margaret asked one af-ternoon.

They were in the front parlor, moving pieces of furniture so they could wash the baseboards behind them. Mr. Rainwater had paused on his way out to tell them that he would be back by suppertime. Through the front window, Margaret had watched him drive away, then posed the question to Ella.

She responded with feigned disinterest. "Going on?"

"With Mr. Rainwater. Where's he off to here lately?"

"I don't know, Margaret. He doesn't tell me, and it's none of my business. Or yours," she added pointedly.

The maid applied her damp rag to the baseboard. "I'm thinkin' he might have a lady friend tucked away somewhere."

"He might."

Margaret snuffled and shook her head. "You know what the mens is like."

Ella let that go without comment.

A few days later, she ran into Lola Thompson in the post office. Lola's youngest child was riding on her hip. She had an-other by the hand, and she was juggling a handful of mail that she'd just retrieved from her box.

When Ella greeted her, she was as ready as ever with a wide grin. "I got a letter from my cousin. She's expecting again. I swear. As if they didn't have enough mouths to feed." She used the mail to fan her round, flushed face.

"You've been on my mind a lot," Ella told her. "How have you been?"

"Oh, fine."

"Ollie?"

"He's mending fences. Plugging up holes in the roof. Work-ing toward the day he can start another herd. We're not making anything, but we're not spending much, either. We're carrying on best we can. What choice do we have?"

"I admire your resilience."

Lola chuckled. "I've had my dark hours. Wouldn't be human if I didn't. But I try not to let on in front of Ollie and the kids."

"Anytime you'd like to talk, call me or come by."

Lola snorted. "Like you need my big self crying on your shoulder, what with your backward boy, and you being all alone, running that house by yourself. If anybody should be admired, Ella, it's you, not me."

She didn't take exception to Lola's description of Solly, knowing there was no malice intended. "I would welcome a visit with you. Anytime."

Lola let go of her child's hand and touched Ella's. "I appreciate that. Sometimes talking to another woman is just the thing. We females understand each other, don't we?"

Ella nodded.

Lola reflected a moment, then said, "I guess it's the same with men, though. I'm glad Ollie's come to know Mr. Rainwater right good. He came along just when Ollie needed a friend. Their talks have helped Ollie, I think."

Ella's heart gave a little bump. "Mr. Rainwater's been having talks with Ollie?"

"Before and after their meetings. Sometimes he stays over after everybody else has left, or he comes early."

Ella stared at her with bewilderment. "Lola, what are you talking about? What meetings?"

"You know." She bobbed her heavy eyebrows, then glanced around to see if anyone was close enough to overhear. Leaning toward Ella, she whispered, "The *meetings*."

<hr/>

His headlights cut through the darkness even before he turned his car onto the street. Nearby houses were dark. It was past bedtime for most folks. The town was quiet except for a freight train that rumbled through without slowing down or stopping.

Mr. Rainwater had left the house while Ella was working in the kitchen after dinner. The spinsters played cards for a while, then retired. Mr. Hastings, dead tired from another trip, went upstairs directly after dinner. Ella put Solly to bed, saw Margaret off with a pail of pinto beans and two pans of corn bread to dispense in shantytown, then went out onto the porch to wait for her boarder's return.

Now Mr. Rainwater parked his car behind Mr. Hastings's, turned off the headlights, cut the engine. He came up the walk, climbed the steps, and was reaching for the handle of the screened door when she said, "Good evening, Mr. Rainwater."

He drew up short and turned toward her as he whipped off his hat. "Mrs. Barron. I didn't see you." He walked toward the rocking chair where she sat. "I hope you weren't waiting up for me so you could lock the door."

"I was waiting for you, but not so I could lock the door. In fact, I may wish I had locked you out."

His head went back an inch or two as if he were dodging a blow. "I beg your pardon?"

"Where have you been?"

He paused for several beats, then said, "May I sit down?"

She gave a curt nod. He took the chair nearest hers, even pulling it a few inches closer to the rocker.

In response to that, she moved her knees, directing them away from him. "Before you say anything, Mr. Rainwater, you should know that I saw Lola today. She mentioned secret meetings taking place at their house, assuming that I knew the purpose of them."

"They're not always at the Thompsons' house."

His composure was infuriating.

"Where these meetings are conducted isn't the point. What *kind* of meetings are they? What's the purpose of them?"

Her voice had gone up in volume. He cut his eyes toward the yard, beyond it to the house across the road, then glanced over his shoulder toward the hedge of oleander bushes that separated her property from her neighbor's.

His caution only heightened her misgivings, but she lowered her voice to a whisper. "Please don't think I care about your comings and goings for any reason other than that you're living in my house and eating at my table. I believe that entitles me to know if you're into something dangerous or criminal."

"I assure you it's not criminal."

"But dangerous?"

"I hope it won't become so."

"You still haven't answered my question. What's the purpose of the meetings?"

He placed his hat on his knee and leaned toward her. "This drought relief program to buy livestock was designed specifically to help people in dire straits, not cause them more grief. People suffering hard times shouldn't also have their houses riddled with bullets, their property damaged or destroyed, and their children threatened. Like what happened to the Pritchetts and the Thompsons. We want to stop it."

" 'We.' Who?"

"Me, Ollie, Brother Calvin. He's rallied men in shantytown, Negroes and whites, those who were beaten to within an inch of their lives. Remember the man with the three children whose wife had just died?"

She nodded, remembering that she'd seen Mr. Rainwater talking with him.

"His name's Emmett Sprule. He's been in the shantytown for a long time, so he knows a lot of people. Pritchett signed on. He's brought in all his lodge friends, even deacons in his church."

"Brought them in to do what?"

"We've got a network in place now, a relay system. When it comes time for a farmer's or rancher's herd to be bought and culled, he sends word. It's spread through the system we've worked out. We all drop what we're doing and converge on the place. We can't change the rules of the program." He flashed a grin that showed up white in the darkness. "We might bend them a little and get some fresh meat or a soup bone to those people while no one's looking. But short of that, we can certainly stop Conrad Ellis and his cronies from doing their meanness."

"Conrad's wild. He and his gang are armed and reckless."

"We're armed, too. But we're not wild or reckless. We're organized. And there are more of us than there are of them. If we make a stand, I think those thugs will back down. Men who've lost their livelihoods, their homes, men who've been beaten down will start feeling like men again."

The idea behind their organization was noble, but she feared men from shantytown armed with sticks, and church deacons with Christian decency as their armor, wouldn't pose much of a threat to Conrad and his heavily armed, drunken, violent friends.

"It's the law's job to protect people and property," she argued. "Why don't you send a committee to appeal to the sheriff?"

"Anderson is scared of the Ellises. He won't cross Conrad's father, who bankrolled his election."

It was true, but she wondered how Mr. Rainwater, an outsider, had come by that information. When she asked him, he said, "Ollie told me Sheriff Anderson was gutless and on the take, and everyone confirmed it. Brother Calvin said he and his deputies stood by and watched Conrad and his friends beat up those people out at Pritchett's place, remember?"

"I remember very well. Which only proves my point." She pulled her lower lip through her teeth. "Please don't get involved, Mr. Rainwater."

"I already am."

"This isn't your town. You've only just met these people. I'm surprised they'd even have the nerve to invite you to join them." She stopped suddenly. When she next spoke, her words came out in a slow, measured cadence. "Who organized these men? Who devised this system of communication, this relay?"

His steady gaze didn't falter.

"You did."

He said nothing.

Ella's breath caught in her throat. *"Why?"*

"It needed to be done."

"Not by you!"

"Why not by me?"

"It's not your fight. You're not a rancher or dairy farmer. You don't live in shantytown. You didn't get clubbed by those hoodlums. You're not involved."

"I involved myself."

"Well, you shouldn't have. It's a dangerous situation. Sheriff Anderson could arrest you."

He looked amused. "For what? Meeting with friends?"

"For anything. For spitting on the sidewalk. If the Ellises tell him to put you behind bars, he will. Or worse, they may leave him out of it and come after you themselves."

"Come after me?" he repeated, again looking amused. "And do what?"

"Whatever they have a mind to! Do not underestimate Conrad, Mr. Rainwater. He could hurt you, and he would."

"I'm not afraid of him."

"Well, I am. And you should be. Stay out of his way, and out of this business."

"I'm sorry, I can't. It's too late to back out, even if I wanted to, and I don't want to."

"I don't understand you. Truly I don't. Why risk your life—" She bit back her words, stopping before finishing the thought.

Mr. Rainwater smiled wanly and gave a small shrug. "Exactly."

ELEVEN

They said no more about it that night. Realizing the futility of arguing with a man willing to cut even shorter his short life expectancy, Ella had gone inside and straight to her room, trusting that Mr. Rainwater would remember to latch the door when he came in.

At breakfast the following morning, they exchanged polite nods but didn't speak. At midmorning, he came out into the backyard, where she was hanging towels on the clothesline. Solly was sitting in the dirt, drumming a wooden spoon against the bottom of an upturned metal bucket. Margaret was in the shed feeding wet clothes into the wringer.

As Mr. Rainwater approached, he touched the brim of his hat. "Good morning, Mrs. Barron."

"Good morning."

"We didn't finish our conversation last night."

"I can't tell you how to live your life." She pushed a clothespin over the corner of a towel, securing it to the line, then turned to him, raising her hand to shade her eyes against the sun. "But I won't allow you to bring any trouble into my house."

"That's the last thing I want to do."

"That may not be your intention, but that doesn't mean it won't happen. People know you live here. Your involvement in this business puts Solly and me, everyone in this house, at risk."

"I would leave before I let anything bad happen to you."

He said it with such conviction, Ella glanced uneasily toward the shed, certain that Margaret was doing her best to eavesdrop even though she was pretending not to as she cranked the handle of the wringer. Probably Margaret already knew what was going on, especially since Brother Calvin was one of the ringleaders. But Ella didn't want anything she and Mr. Rainwater said to each other repeated.

Her gaze came back to him. "I'll hold you to that."

"If you ask me to move out, I will."

"Do you have a firearm?"

"No."

"Because I don't want guns in my house. Solly—"

"I don't have one."

"And I don't want any of these meetings conducted on my property."

"I would never suggest it."

She gave him a long look, then bent toward the basket on the ground and took another wet towel from it, shaking it until it snapped. "I still think it's foolhardy for you to become involved in this when you don't even have a stake in it."

He removed a clothespin from the cloth bag hanging on

the line and extended it to her. "But I do have a stake in it, Mrs. Barron. A big stake."

She looked at him inquisitively as she took the clothespin from him.

"I'd like the time I have left to count for something."

He backed away, then stepped around the basket of laundry and Solly, and headed toward the front of the house.

"Mr. Rainwater?"

She called out to him without thinking and was embarrassed by her spontaneity. She was aware of Margaret, well within earshot. Aware also that she was clutching the wet towel against her chest. But it was too late now. He had turned back and was looking at her expectantly.

"Take care."

He smiled and touched the brim of his hat again. "Thank you. I will."

Holding Solly by the hand, Ella entered the sanctuary and found them seats on one of the back pews. Each Sunday she timed her arrival to be a few minutes late, during the singing of a hymn or when heads were bowed in prayer, in order to avoid the other churchgoers, who stared at Solly with curiosity, sometimes with apprehension, often with compassion that bordered on pity, all of which Ella scorned and didn't want Solly subjected to.

He looked like an angel today. She'd dressed him in a white linen shirt and matching shorts, which she'd bought at a rummage sale last summer, hoping that by this year he would have grown into them. His shorts attached to his shirt with large round buttons. His kneesocks were spotless; she'd polished his shoes last night. This morning, she'd managed to rake a comb through his pale hair several times before he began squealing and flapping his hands at the sides of his head.

She went to great pains every Sunday to dress him up, knowing the effort was wasted. No one noticed how well he was turned out, only that he was different, that he wasn't "right." Which was all the more reason for his appearance to be superior.

When they were settled in the pew, an usher kindly offered her a hymnal opened to the song being led by the twenty-voice choir, which, despite the two basses and one baritone, always sounded tinny.

She'd brought along a small bag of empty spools to keep Solly occupied during the service. Prayers were said, more hymns were sung, the offering plates were passed. The pastor began his sermon.

This morning's message wasn't all that inspiring. Ella's attention began to drift, and so did her gaze. As it moved across the congregation, she spotted Mr. Rainwater. He was seated at the end of the pew, on the outside aisle, about midway between where she sat and the altar. He was looking directly at the minister, so to Ella, his face was in profile. For once the errant lock of hair that usually defied his hair tonic had remained in place. She was taken again by how pronounced his cheekbones were, how well defined his chin was.

He had an aspect of quiet intensity, attesting to his total absorption in whatever he was looking at or listening to. But his eyes were never passive. Even when they were still, there was industry in their depths. Like that of a spring-fed stream, the surface remained relatively calm despite the undercurrents.

She was surprised to see him. To her knowledge, this was

the first time he'd attended services. He was seated with Dr. and Mrs. Kincaid, who was presently admonishing one of her restless sons with a warning glare to sit still and stop pestering his brother.

The Ellises were occupying their customary pew, the second on the right-hand side of the center aisle. No one else would dare sit in their pew. If a visitor did so unknowingly, another seat was suggested to him.

Even from the back and sitting still, Conrad looked pugnacious. Perhaps because his large head sat upon his wide shoulders with barely an inch of neck supporting it. His hair was as curly and dense as wool, covering his head like a tightly fitted cap. It added to his belligerent look.

Mr. Ellis sat beside him. He was a smaller man than his son, much less brawny, but he led with his chin, his head jutting slightly forward of his shoulders, in a way that looked aggressive, competitive, and combatant.

Although Mrs. Ellis, decked out this morning in pink voile, was the best dressed woman in town, she was not admired or well liked. The general consensus was that she put on airs and was stingy with her contributions of time and money to charities and civic organizations. She hosted social events in her home, but only for her fancy friends in Waco, never for local women.

It seemed to Ella that everyone in the church heaved a sigh of relief when the pastor finally wound down and closed the sermon with a prayer. At the end of it, he beseeched God to give direction to the misguided. It seemed an odd note on which to conclude the service, but it was explained when Mr. Ellis said a resounding, "Amen," from his pew.

"I think Ellis wrote the closing prayer."

Recognizing the voice, Ella turned. Mr. Rainwater was beside her, but his gaze was on the family currently talking to the pastor. As they watched, Mr. Ellis clapped the minister on the shoulder as he enthusiastically pumped his right hand. Mrs. Ellis fanned her face with a lace hankie that matched her dress. Conrad, looking bored, walked away from the group and lit a cigarette.

"I wouldn't put it past him," Ella said. "Mr. Ellis is a very influential member of the church."

"Was it just me, or did you detect a subtle warning in that prayer? Who do you suppose determines who is and who isn't 'misguided'?"

She knew Mr. Rainwater's question was rhetorical, so she didn't venture an answer.

He looked down at Solly, who was standing docilely at her side, staring at the panes in the stained-glass window. "I didn't hear a peep out of this young man. Can't say the same for Murdy's boys."

Ella laughed. "They're a handful. But today Solly was very good." She was aware of eyes on them, especially when Mr. Rainwater politely cupped her elbow as they started down the steep front steps of the church. When they reached ground level, she slipped her arm free but covered the move by saying, "I haven't seen you here before."

"First time."

"What did you think?"

"Boring sermon."

"Even the diehards were snoozing this morning." They smiled at each other, then she ducked her head, grateful for the brim of her hat, which helped conceal her face. "Margaret's made a pork roast and two pies for Sunday dinner. I'll see you then." Pulling Solly along behind her, she turned and headed down the sidewalk.

"I'll walk you to your car."

"We came on foot this morning."

"Then I'll drive you home."

"Thank you, Mr. Rainwater, but we have a . . . an errand to attend to."

"I'll drive you wherever you need to go."

"Our errand is here, actually."

He looked toward where she indicated: the cemetery that was adjacent to the church.

"I brought some cuttings from the yard for my parents' . . . For my parents." Because of his prognosis, she felt too uncomfortable with the subject of burial to say the word *graves*.

"Where are they? The cuttings," he said, when she showed her confusion over whether he meant where were her parents or where were the flowers.

"I put them in the shade before we went into the church so they would stay fresh."

He made a motion with his head for her to lead on.

"You don't have to stay with us," she said.

"Do you mind if I do?"

"Not at all. It's just awfully hot today."

"It's hot every day. Heat doesn't bother me that much."

She saw no way of dissuading him without drawing the attention of lingerers still in the churchyard. Without further argument she led him around the corner of the building to the deep shade, where the bouquet was where she'd left it. Still in the Mason jar of water were colorful zinnias, a pair of creamy gardenias, and some late-blooming yellow roses, which so far had defied the summer weather.

Mr. Rainwater picked up the jar. "Very fragrant."

"I thought it was nice."

Together they covered the distance to the cemetery and went through the iron picket gate. He didn't seem upset to be in a place so remindful of death. He read with obvious interest the names and dates on the headstones as they moved among them on their way to the plot shared by her parents.

She let go of Solly's hand and took the jar of flowers from Mr. Rainwater, then knelt down and set the jar in the center of the headstone on which were engraved their names, their dates of birth and death, and a simple inscription: UNITED IN HEAVEN FOR ETERNITY.

Flanking their graves were two smaller ones with only brass plaques, flush to the ground, designating the individuals buried there. Ella removed two roses from the jar and laid one on each of these graves.

"Your twin brothers?"

She nodded, wondering if Mr. Rainwater noticed her exclusion from the family plot. No contingency had been made for her interment.

She pulled up several weeds, rearranged the flowers in the jar, then brushed off her hands and stood up.

"Do you come here every Sunday?" he asked.

"Once a month, maybe."

"Is your husband also buried here?"

The question was unexpected. "No, he isn't," she said as

she reached for Solly's hand and started quickly retracing their path to the gate. "He wasn't from Gilead. He was born in a small town in the Panhandle and grew up there. He liked the wide open spaces of the plains. He told me on more than one occasion that he wished to be buried out there."

"I see."

They walked on, but when they reached the gate, Ella stopped. Mr. Rainwater did likewise. By now, even the stragglers had left. The doors to the sanctuary were closed. Only Mr. Rainwater's car remained parked in front of the church. The sun was reflecting off its windshield, radiating blinding shafts of light.

A lone woman, whom Ella recognized as one of her former schoolteachers, was walking away from them along the cracked and buckled sidewalk, carrying her handbag in one gloved hand, her large black Bible in the other. "Miss" Winnie had been a childless widow for as long as Ella had known her, and she wore the same hat to church every Sunday, regardless of the season. Perhaps she was very proud of the feather that curled around the crown of it. She spoke of her many cats as though they were children.

Something twisted inside Ella. She wished she'd seen her former teacher earlier so she could have invited her to join them for Sunday dinner. Otherwise, Miss Winnie would no doubt eat alone, then spend the rest of the day in solitude, with only her cats for company.

"My husband didn't die, Mr. Rainwater."

He remained silent and unmoving at her side, as still as the oak trees shading the graves. Eventually she turned to him. "I don't know why Dr. Kincaid told you that I was a widow. To spare me embarrassment, I suppose."

She glanced down at Solly. He seemed fascinated by the even placement of the pickets in the fence. He swayed back and forth as he studied them. Rays of sunlight speared through the branches of the nearest tree, shining on selected strands of Solly's hair, making them appear almost translucent. Ella lightly stroked them with her fingertip. He jerked his head away from her touch.

"The truth is, my husband abandoned us six years ago. One day while I was out, he packed his belongings and left. I have no idea where he went. Back to the Panhandle perhaps. Or to another state. I don't know. He didn't leave a note, nothing. I never heard from him again."

She turned her gaze back to the man beside her. "You've been kind to Solly and to me. In good conscience, I couldn't continue lying to you." Before he could say anything, she ushered Solly through the gate, having every intention of walking home.

But Mr. Rainwater went ahead of her and opened the passenger door of his car, motioning her in. She hesitated but saw no reason to refuse his offer of a lift. The visit to the cemetery had taken time, and her boarders would be expecting their dinner at two o'clock sharp.

Placing Solly in the middle of the seat, she climbed in after him. Mr. Rainwater closed her door, walked around the hood, and got in. He started the motor, then let it idle as he stared through the windshield for several moments. Finally he turned his head. She braced herself for the dreaded questions.

"What kinds of pies?"

"What?"

"You said Margaret made two pies for dinner. What kind?"

For six years she had withstood the gossip, speculation,

insinuation, blatant nosiness, and sympathy of everyone who knew her. To newcomers in town, she was identified as the woman with the retarded boy whose husband had deserted them. She had borne the humiliation and pity with as much fortitude as she could muster.

Mr. Rainwater had subjected her to neither.

With emotion in her throat, she replied, "It's a surprise."

TWELVE

"It wasn't just a stomach flu, was it?"

Ella and Margaret were in the kitchen, pickling cucumbers, okra pods, and watermelon rind. It was hot work, and there were no shortcuts to the process. The vegetables and rinds had to be thoroughly washed, sliced, and blanched. The Mason jars and their lids had to be boiled. The spices and vinegar were simmered together to achieve the best flavors.

Everything in the kitchen was steaming.

Including Ella, who pushed back coils of hair that had escaped her bun. She looked at Margaret, who was ladling a hot vinegar mixture redolent with dill over the cucumber spears she had packed tightly into a jar. Ella was prepared to play dumb or fib in reply to Margaret's question, but when her loyal maid looked back at her, she knew that duplicity was pointless.

Margaret knew, or at least sensed, that Mr. Rainwater suffered an ailment, and she hadn't been fooled by the explanation they'd provided the day Dr. Kincaid had been summoned to the house to treat him.

"No, Margaret. It wasn't just a stomach flu."

"He don't eat much. Less ever' day. I thought it was just the heat." Margaret set the seal on the rim of the jar, then twisted on the ring. Wiping her hands on her apron, she turned to Ella. "Is he bad sick?"

"Very bad."

Ella didn't need to elaborate. Her tone spoke volumes. Tears filled Margaret's eyes. "Poor, poor soul. How long?"

"No one knows that for sure."

"A year?"

Ella shook her head. "Not that long."

Margaret raised her apron to catch a sob in the hem of it.

"But please don't say anything about it to anyone, especially not to him. He doesn't want anyone to know. He doesn't want a fuss made. Don't act any differently toward him. Promise me you won't."

"I won't," Margaret mumbled as she blotted her eyes. "But it ain't gonna be easy, 'cause I think a lot of him. He's a gentleman, about the most decent white man I know."

"If you feel that way about him, the nicest thing you can do for him is to treat him normally. Don't let on like you know."

"Yes, ma'am."

Ella began slicing cucumber disks for her bread and butter pickles.

"Miss Ella? Did you know? Before that day we had to call the doctor?"

"I knew before he moved in."

"You a good woman."

Holding her knife poised above her chop board, Ella raised her head and looked through the window over the drainboard. Steam had fogged the windowpane. As she watched, it condensed into an iridescent bead of water that trickled down the glass like a raindrop, or a tear.

After that conversation with Margaret, she began taking particular notice of Mr. Rainwater's appetite, or lack thereof. She monitored how much food he left on his plate after each meal. One night as she was clearing the table, she asked if the meat loaf hadn't been to his liking.

"It was delicious, Mrs. Barron. But my eyes were bigger than my stomach. I took too large a portion."

But from then on, he did better toward cleaning his plate. She was heartened, until one evening when she saw how little he served himself. His portion of chicken and dumplings was less than what she'd dished up for Solly.

She didn't mention it to him in front of the Dunne sisters or Mr. Hastings, who was disappointed when Mr. Rainwater declined a game of chess and, saying he preferred to read that night, excused himself and went upstairs.

Before going to bed, Ella decided she should check on him. Rarely did she go upstairs once her boarders had retired, feeling they deserved their privacy. But knowing that Mr. Rainwater had suffered in silence through one whole night and half a day before she discovered his misery, she felt justified in breaking her rule. She told herself that if no light shone beneath his door, she wouldn't disturb him, and no one ever need know she'd been there. But if his light was on, she would verify that he was comfortable.

As soon as she reached the landing, she saw that his door was the only one with light shining beneath it. Keeping her footsteps light, so as not to disturb the others or alert them to her presence, she made her way down the dark hallway to his room, where she tapped softly on the door.

"Yes?"

"It's me, Mr. Rainwater," she whispered. "Are you all right?"

"Yes."

She waited for him to say more. When he didn't, she asked if she could come in.

"Yes."

She pushed open the door. He was sitting on the side of the bed, but it was apparent that he'd been lying on it seconds earlier. The pillow bore the imprint of his head, and his hair was tousled. He was dressed, although he had removed his coat and necktie, and had lowered his suspenders. His cuffs were loose around his wrists. His shoes were on the floor beside the bed, but he was still wearing his socks.

His skin looked pale and waxy, but that could have been attributed to the harsh glow of the reading lamp on his nightstand. It also turned his eye sockets into dark caverns, preventing her from seeing into his eyes.

She stepped into the room but left the door open. "I hope I'm not disturbing you."

"Not at all."

"I wanted to ask if you thought I should write to one of those schools for special children that Dr. Kincaid recommended."

He looked at her for a long moment, then stood up. "You didn't believe me."

"Pardon?"

"You didn't believe me when I told you that I was all right. That's why you came in."

She smiled self-consciously. "I confess."

"You're a terrible liar."

"I'm aware of that."

"It's not a bad quality, being so honest you can't conceal a lie." They smiled across at each other. She asked, "Are you?"

"Am I a good liar?"

"Are you all right?"

"Yes."

She nodded toward the book he held in one hand, his index finger marking his place. "You really did come up early so you could read your book."

"A *Farewell to Arms*. Have you read it?"

"I've wanted to. I don't have much time for leisure reading."

"It's excellent."

"Doesn't it have a sad ending?"

"Sad but beautiful, they say. I'll let you know."

Feeling awkward now, she backed away and reached for the doorknob. "I apologize for the intrusion. I noticed you didn't eat well tonight. I wanted to make sure that you weren't . . . that you were resting well."

"I appreciate your concern, but I'm fine."

"Then good night, Mr. Rainwater."

"Good night, Mrs. Barron."

She pulled the door closed, but for several moments she huddled in the dark hallway, her hand gripping the doorknob, her heart clenching with indecision, wondering if she'd been right to pretend that she hadn't seen on the bedside table, along with his gold cuff links and pocket watch, the syringe and vial of pain medication.

The following morning, she was still wrestling with uncertainty. Should she, or should she not, notify Dr. Kincaid, whom she had promised to send for at the least sign of discomfort from Mr. Rainwater. She was on the verge of making the call when he joined the Dunne sisters at the dining table.

"What's for breakfast this morning, ladies?"

"Pancakes," Miss Violet informed him.

"My favorite."

"Mine, too."

Not to be outdone by her sister, Miss Pearl said, "And the most delicious honeydew melon we've had all season."

"That must be it then."

"Must be what, Mr. Rainwater?"

"The source of that special glow you two have this morning," he said, teasing them with a wink. "Honeydew melon!"

They tittered, and Miss Pearl accused him of being a naughty flirt. He met Ella's eyes as she poured coffee into his cup. "Good morning, Mrs. Barron."

"I hope you had a restful night, Mr. Rainwater."

"Slept like a baby."

But the deep shadows beneath his eyes made her wonder if he were, in fact, a better liar than she. He did justice to his breakfast, reassuring her somewhat. After the meal, he took a box of dominoes, a deck of cards, and Solly out onto the front porch. They stayed an hour. When he brought Solly back to her, he smiled down at the boy. "Good job, Solly."

"Did he do something special?"

"Everything he does is special, Mrs. Barron."

"Yes, it is." After a beat, she said, "What I asked you last night wasn't just a ruse to check on you. I'd like your opinion."

"About the special schools?"

"Should I write to them and ask about their curriculums?"

"What would it hurt?"

"Nothing, I suppose, although I don't think I could ever bring myself to send Solly away."

"Until you know more, you can't make an informed decision. By his own admission Murdy knows very little about children like Solly. But these schools may be able to provide answers and guidance."

Making up her mind, she said, "I'll send out some inquiries."

"Good." Looking happy about her decision, he excused himself and continued down the central hallway toward the staircase. When he was about halfway up, she called after him, "Can I get you anything, Mr. Rainwater?"

He stopped, turned. "Like what?"

"A glass of iced tea?"

"No thank you."

"It was awfully hot out on the porch."

"I'm not thirsty."

He took the next few steps, a bit slower, she thought.

"Are you sure you're feeling all right? You look—"

He spun around. "I'm *fine*."

It was the first time she'd ever heard him raise his voice, the first time he'd ever displayed a temper, and it came as such a shock that for a moment she couldn't think of what to say or do. So she took Solly by the hand and led him into the kitchen, letting the door swing closed behind them.

❧⟨━━⊷⊷⊶⊶━━⟩❧

After lunch, she decided that she and Solly would walk to town. As much as they needed the exercise, she believed that time away from the house would do them both good.

The heat was unrelenting, however. Her dress was damp with perspiration by the time they reached the store. Its comparably cool interior felt good, and Solly was content to watch the circulating ceiling fan, so she dawdled among the shelves as she checked items off her shopping list. Too soon she was done.

"Is that it for today, Mrs. Barron?"

"Yes, thank you, Mr. Randall. Oh, wait, two cold Dr Peppers, please."

The grocer glanced at Solly, who was standing at her side, bobbing his head. "Sure thing. Want me to uncap them for you?"

"Please."

A large hand came into view from her right side and slapped two nickels onto the counter. "My treat." When Ella turned, she was looking into Conrad Ellis's face. His leer was more disfiguring than the unfortunate birthmark.

"Long time no see, Ella."

"Hello, Conrad."

He assessed her appearance in a way that was insulting and made her skin crawl. "You're lookin' good. Staying trim." She didn't say anything to that. His grin only widened over her apparent embarrassment. Turning to Mr. Randall, he said, "The Dr Peppers are on me."

"Thank you, Conrad," she said crisply, "but Mr. Randall will add them to my account."

Conrad reached across the counter and socked the grocer on the arm. "Mr. Randall will let me buy you a soda water, won't you, Mr. Randall?"

The grocer gave Ella a weak smile. "I've already closed out your tab, Mrs. Barron." He hadn't, but he obviously didn't want to haggle with Conrad. He swept the nickels off the counter, then quickly turned and took two of the soft drinks from the metal chest. He shook ice chips off the bottles and hastily uncapped them, then set them on the counter. "Thanks for your business. I'll have your purchases boxed and sent right over by Margaret's boy."

"Thank you."

After looking askance at Conrad, he disappeared into his storeroom.

Conrad was a bulky presence she tried to ignore as she took Solly's hand and headed for the door. There was no one else in the store, which she was glad of, because she didn't want any witnesses to this encounter. At the same time, since Mr. Randall's retreat, she was alone with Conrad, which made her distinctly uncomfortable and even a little afraid.

As she stepped past him, he said, "Hey, you forgot your drinks."

"I've changed my mind."

"Aw, now. Don't be like that, Ella." He hooked her arm, which she yanked back immediately. He laughed. "What's the matter? No time to chat with an old friend?"

"Not today. I need to get home."

"You still cooking and cleaning for other people?"

"I'm running a business."

"Is that what they call making beds and mopping floors these days? Running a business?" He snorted with derision. "You're too good for that, Ella. Don't you ever get a hankering for something better?"

"No."

"Bet you do," he drawled.

She tried to go around him, but he executed a quick side-step and blocked her. "Let me by, Conrad."

"You ever hear from that sorry husband of yours?"

Again she tried to go around him, but he was too quick for her, especially since she had Solly in tow.

"He just up and ran off, didn't he? On account of your boy here. I guess he couldn't take his kid being the town idiot."

Ella seethed as he bent at the waist and put himself on an eye level with Solly, who stared through him.

"What's the matter with him, anyway?" He waved his hand in front of Solly's face and said in a falsetto, "Yoo-hoo! Anybody home?"

"Stop that!" Ella tried to push Conrad aside, but it was like trying to shove a railroad car. He pressed his hand over hers, trapping it against his chest. She struggled to pull it free, but he mashed it beneath his. "Let me go!"

Chuckling over her futile efforts, he said, "You always did have sass, Ella. I liked that about you. Even your husband running off hasn't got the best of you, has it? Shame about your kid, though. Now that I've seen him up close, it just goes to show you can't believe everything you hear. What I heard was that he duh . . . duh . . . drools, and is all the time sh . . . sh . . . shittin' his p . . . p . . . pants."

"You really should try to correct that stutter, Mr. Ellis."

Mr. Rainwater pulled open the store's screened door and strolled in. Ella almost cried out in relief upon seeing him. Conrad released her hand and spun around to see who'd interrupted his bullying.

"Afternoon, Mrs. Barron." Mr. Rainwater doffed the brim

of his hat as he approached, deftly maneuvering himself between her and Conrad.

Their eyes locked. With effort she brought her breathing under control. "Mr. Rainwater."

"Margaret told me you'd come to town. I had an errand to run, so I thought I'd intercept you and offer you and Solly a ride home."

"That's very kind of you. Thank you."

He swept his arm wide, motioning her toward the door and away from Conrad.

But Conrad wasn't going to be ignored. He placed his hand on Mr. Rainwater's shoulder and brought him around to face him. "Hey, I've heard of you."

"I've heard of you, too."

"What I've heard, I don't particularly like."

Mr. Rainwater smiled pleasantly. "Then we also have that in common."

It took Conrad several seconds to process his meaning, and when he did, his eyes narrowed to slits of malice, and his birthmark darkened with anger. "You're Ella's new boarder."

"I'm leasing a room in her house, yes."

Conrad snickered and asked slyly, "What else are you doing there?"

Mr. Rainwater remained stonily silent, although Ella recognized the familiar tightening of his jaw. Conrad outweighed him fifty pounds or more, but Mr. Rainwater didn't seem the least bit intimidated by him. "Please stand aside, Mr. Ellis. We're ready to leave now."

Conrad raised both hands in surrender. "Sure, sure. All I was doing was trying to buy Ella and her idiot kid a soda water. Just trying to do something nice for her." He divided an insinuating look between them. "What I think? I think it's you who's doing something nice for her. Every night? When the lights go out in that big ol' house of hers?" He gave Ella an obscene wink.

Mr. Rainwater gave the small of her back a gentle push toward the door. She could feel the tension in his touch and was comforted by how strong it felt. Placing Solly in front of her, she propelled him toward the door. They had almost reached it when Conrad again clamped his hand on Mr. Rainwater's shoulder.

"You think 'cause you're kin to Doc Kincaid you can go poking your nose into business where it doesn't belong? Well, you can't. Around here we don't like meddlesome outsiders. You hear me? You want to be a busybody, making trouble, getting the niggers and riffraff all stirred up, you go someplace else to do it, and spare me the trouble of having to whip your ass."

THIRTEEN

They said nothing as they walked to his car, but as soon as they were in it, Mr. Rainwater said, "It would tickle him to know he'd upset you."

"I'm not upset."

"You're shaking."

Ella looked down at her hands and realized that he was right. To keep her hands from trembling, she clasped them in her lap.

Solly started screeching.

Just like that he took a sudden and violent objection to his shoes. When she finally was able to hold his feet still, she saw that the toe of one had been scuffed. The smudge was barely discernible, but she kept his shoes polished a glossy black. The mark was enough to bring on a fit. He bucked, kicked, flapped his hands, and all the while emitted an ear-shattering squeal.

She removed the offending shoes. He stopped screeching

but rocked back and forth so vigorously that his head thumped into the upholstered seat. It seemed not to bother him. On the contrary, it seemed to mollify him, so she didn't try to stop it.

When the crisis was over, Mr. Rainwater politely asked if she had any other stops to make in town. She made it plain to him that she did not. She only wanted to get home and, with the help of routine chores, put Conrad and the hateful, disgusting things he'd said out of her mind.

Mr. Rainwater appeared unfazed both by Solly's fit and by the confrontation in the grocery market. His hands were steady on the steering wheel and gearshift as he drove them through town. He even touched the brim of his hat to several people they passed. Ella wished he wouldn't. She felt conspicuous riding in his car now. Anyone seeing her and Solly with him might give credence to gossip that there was something illicit going on under her roof.

To her knowledge, Conrad had been the only one who'd implied such a thing, and nothing Conrad said could be taken for fact, but the mere idea that she and a male boarder were the subjects of lewd speculation made her ill.

"He's not worth fretting over," Mr. Rainwater said quietly.

"His fits are getting worse, not better. More intense."

"Not Solly. Conrad Ellis."

"I disagree. Conrad is very much worth fretting over. If you could have heard the ugly things he said about Solly—"

"I did, as I was coming in. The man is a bully, a moron, and if you let him make you angry or upset, you're giving him exactly what he's after. Your best defense against him is to ignore him."

"As you did." The words came out sharply, almost like a reproof.

He looked at her but replied in his typically calm manner. "I couldn't ignore the things he said. I simply declined to take issue with them, knowing that's exactly what he wanted me to do. If I'd challenged what he suggested about us, it would have given him an opportunity to lay into me."

"He could break you in half."

He smiled. "Yes. In a fistfight I would most definitely lose. But he didn't fight me, did he?"

She thought of the steely resolve she'd seen in Mr. Rainwater's eyes as he stared down Conrad. Apparently Conrad had seen it, too. He had removed his hand from Mr. Rainwater's shoulder and had even taken a step back. He was aggressive by nature, and his parents had cultivated in him feelings of superiority and entitlement. She didn't remember a time when Conrad had walked away from a fight.

Could it possibly be that Conrad had been afraid of a quality he'd detected in Mr. Rainwater's eyes? Perhaps the strength of purpose of a man who had nothing to lose and nothing more to fear? Whatever the reason, Conrad's brute strength and belligerence had tucked tail and retreated from it.

As soon as Mr. Rainwater brought the car to a stop in front of the house, she scrambled out, pulling Solly along with her. She didn't want Mr. Rainwater coming around to open the car door for her or doing anything chivalrous that would validate rumors of a romance.

She entered through the front door and didn't stop her steady march until she reached the kitchen, where Margaret and her son, Jimmy, were unloading the grocery items he'd delivered.

As soon as Margaret saw her, she planted a fist on her jutting hip bone and smacked the back of Jimmy's head with her other hand. "I done eat him out good for leaving you in the store alone with that white trash. And I can tell by your flushed face that somethin' bad happened."

"We're fine, Margaret."

"Well, it's a wonder," she huffed. "That Ellis boy was born mean, and just got meaner when he had to give you up. He ain't got over you turnin' him down flat."

Hearing motion behind her, Ella turned. Mr. Rainwater had followed her into the kitchen, Solly's shoes in his hand. He divided a curious look between her and Margaret, landing on her. "You left these in the car, Mrs. Barron."

She snatched the shoes from him. "Thank you, Mr. Rainwater."

He looked at her more closely, but she turned away.

Margaret said, "This is my boy, Jimmy. Jimmy, Mr. Rainwater."

The two acknowledged the introduction, then Jimmy scuttled out the back door, as though grateful to have escaped his mother's wrath.

"Margaret," Mr. Rainwater said, "if I pick the peaches myself, could I bribe you into making a cobbler for dessert tonight?"

"Shoot! You don't have to bribe me. I'd be pleasured to do it."

He picked ripe peaches from the tree in the southwest corner of Ella's yard. Margaret baked the cobbler. But Mr. Rainwater wasn't there for dessert to eat it.

The phone rang during the dinner hour. Ella answered.

"Ella, it's Ollie. Let me speak to David, please."

So it was *David* now. But sensing urgency, she asked if something was wrong.

"If he's there, just put him on, please."

"Hold on." Mystified, and not a little troubled by the tone

of his voice, Ella returned to the dining room, where her boarders were having their main course. "Mr. Rainwater, you have a telephone call."

He stood immediately and dropped his napkin beside his plate. Excusing himself to the others, he stepped past Ella and into the hallway, walking quickly toward the table beneath the stairs, which the telephone shared with the deposit box for rent money.

"Who is it?" he asked her over his shoulder.

"Ollie Thompson."

He glanced back at her as he picked up the two components of the telephone. "Ollie?"

He listened for what seemed like an eternity but was actually only a few seconds. "I'll be right there," he said into the mouthpiece, then disconnected immediately.

He replaced the earpiece in the hook and returned the telephone to the table. Stepping around Ella again, he headed for the front door.

"What is it? Where are you going? What's happening?"

"I'll fill you in when I get back." He yanked his hat from the hall tree on his way out. He didn't look back.

Time plodded by.

When she returned to the dining room without him, the Dunne sisters were all aflutter. "Is something wrong?" Miss Violet asked.

"Mr. Rainwater has been called to the home of a friend. Are you ready for your cobbler and cream?" Her calmness was faked, of course, but it allayed the sisters' concern.

"It's like him, isn't it, to rush to the aid of a friend at a moment's notice," Miss Pearl said. "He didn't even wait to finish his dinner. He's such a nice young man."

"And smart," Mr. Hastings said as he helped himself to another ear of corn. "Knows my chess moves before I make them. Pass the butter, please, Miss Pearl."

As soon as dinner was over, Ella left Margaret to deal with the cleanup and took Solly to their rooms. His fit in the car that afternoon seemed to have sapped him of energy. He was docile when she gave him a sponge bath and dressed him in pajamas. Ordinarily she would have been dodging flailing limbs.

She was relieved to discover that her boarders had retired early, too. The twin parlors were empty and dark by the time she returned to the kitchen, where Margaret was wrapping a rag around her index finger.

"Oh dear, what happened?"

"I cut myself with that blamed ol' butcher knife."

"It's still bleeding. Should you have Dr. Kincaid take a look?"

"Naw, ain't nothing a little coal oil won't help. I'll bandage it soon as I get home."

"Go on now."

"The dishes ain't did."

"You can't wash or dry dishes with a bloody finger."

Margaret put up token protests, but Ella entreated her to leave and see to her injury. Eventually she did, apologizing for leaving Ella with so much work still to be done. Actually, Ella didn't mind the seclusion. It had been a grueling day. She didn't want to field any questions from Margaret about the run-in with Conrad, or Mr. Rainwater's mysterious telephone call, which had brought on his abrupt departure from the house.

She ate her own dinner at the kitchen table, but nervousness robbed her of appetite. Not knowing the reason for Ollie Thompson's emergency call had left her sick with worry. According to the kitchen clock, Mr. Rainwater had been gone for over two hours. Where was he, where had he gone, and was he in danger?

She was washing dishes when she heard his car coming down the street. Quickly drying her hands, she ran down the central hallway and unlatched the screened door just as he reached it.

He stepped inside, pulled the door closed and locked it again, then switched out the porch light and the light fixture in the hall. Sensing his tension, Ella stayed still and silent as he looked out across the yard and into the street.

After several minutes, he visibly relaxed. The tension went out of him as he removed his hat and hung it on the hall tree, then turned to her. In a low voice, he asked, "Is any of the cobbler left?"

She led him into the kitchen, realizing as she walked past the staircase that she did so on tiptoe. They didn't speak until the kitchen door had closed behind them. "There's plenty of food left. I can fix you a plate."

He shook his head. "Just the cobbler. After Margaret went to the trouble of making it, I really should eat some. I expected her to still be here."

She told him about the cut finger. "I sent her home. Coffee?"

"Definitely." He hesitated, then said, "I don't suppose you have a secret bottle of . . ."

She shook her head.

"Straight coffee then."

She served him a mug of coffee and a dish of cobbler with a liberal helping of cream, then sat down at the table across from him. "Where did you go? Why did Ollie call?"

"It seemed worse than it turned out to be."

"What happened?"

"They attacked his house. When he called me, it was surrounded by several vehicles. Pickups mostly. He couldn't make out anything except the headlights. They were driving fast and recklessly, round and round the house, knocking down fence posts and Lola's clothesline. One drove into the hog pen, flattened one side of it. The hog got out. It's still missing."

"Who was it?"

"I think we can guess."

"Conrad?"

He blew on his coffee and took a sip. "It was a warning, I think. To Ollie and me and the others. They must've got wind of our organization and the reason for it."

"Or else . . ."

When she paused, he raised his head. "Or else?"

"This is retaliation over our encounter in the store today."

Mr. Rainwater dismissed her concern with a shake of his head. "This had nothing to do with you. Recently, we've had indications that they're onto us. Several times this week, a rancher or farmer got a call that the cattle buyers would be there to evaluate their herd. They were given a day and time. The word was passed, as planned. We assembled. The buyers never showed up."

"The calls were phony."

"But effective." He took another sip of coffee. "Because now, when someone gets a call that the government is ready to do business with him, he doesn't know if it's a false alarm or the real thing."

"Why not call the government office for verification?"

"We tried that, but nothing happens fast in a bureaucracy, especially one in which large sums of Uncle Sam's money are being dispensed. By the time we'd get word that it was a false alarm, men had already wasted hours. My guess is that Conrad and his friends hope to wear us down. They think we'll soon tire of leaving our homes and businesses on the spur of the moment and will give up our plan to protect each other."

"Will you?"

"No." He scraped up the last bit of cream with his spoon, then pushed aside the empty dish. "And if anyone's resolve was wavering, it was reinforced by what those thugs did tonight. When I got there, the pickups were still circling the house. They were throwing bottles at it. I could hear Ollie's kids screaming in fear. All that breaking glass, it sounded like the end of the world. As I said, it seemed worse than it was, but tell that to those frightened kids."

"They must have been terrified."

"Which was the point. But our communication system worked. Angry men began to converge. When Conrad's gang saw they were about to become outnumbered, they struck out across the pasture. A few of our group went after them, but Conrad's bunch turned off their headlights, making it dangerous to follow them. They got away. Is there any coffee left?"

He got up and went to the stove himself, returning with his mug refilled.

"What about Lola and the children? Was anyone hurt?"

"No, thank God. They were just scared half to death. Ollie's father-in-law came and got Lola and the kids. Lola begged Ollie to leave with them, but he stayed. He was afraid those guys might come back, set fire to his barn. Something. A couple of men volunteered to stay with him. Which is noble, but in the meantime their homes and families are left unprotected tonight."

"Where will it end? How?"

Holding her eyes, he said earnestly, "I don't know. But I'm afraid it might get worse before it gets better."

She was afraid of that, too, but she didn't want to admit it, even to herself. "Why do you think that?"

"The line has been drawn in the sand. There are two opposing sides. These things have a way of coming to a head. Especially when the law enforcement agency is indifferent, inept, or flat-out corrupt."

She left the table and went to the sink. The dishwater had grown cold. She drained it and replaced it with hot water, but after turning off the faucet, she curved her hands over the edge of the drainboard, bracing herself against it.

He brought his dessert dish and coffee mug and added them to the stack of dishes to be washed, then slid his hands into his pants pockets. Feeling his gaze on her profile, she turned her head toward him. "I'm afraid."

"I know. I'm sorry."

"It's not your fault."

"It is. You tried to talk me out of becoming involved. You said—"

"I remember clearly what I said, Mr. Rainwater. But my quarrel with Conrad didn't start with you, with this situation. I've always been afraid of him."

He held her gaze until she could bear it no longer. Turning her attention to the sink, she began washing the dishes immersed in the sudsy water. "He pursued me through high school. My mother was thrilled to think of us as sweethearts. Conrad was the richest boy around. She thought he would make an ideal husband. I didn't."

In a separate basin, she rinsed the dishes she had washed.

Out the corner of her eye, she saw Mr. Rainwater take off his suit jacket and drape it over the back of a chair. She stopped what she was doing to watch as he undid his cuff links and rolled up his shirtsleeves. Then he picked up a towel and reached for one of the rinsed dishes.

She put out a hand. "Don't do this."

Gently he moved her hand aside. "Wash."

How could she argue with him without admitting that the mundane chore had suddenly taken on an intimacy that panicked her? It would be far better to assume a neutrality she didn't feel. And when you boiled it down, what harm could come from him drying the dishes?

"You weren't swayed by the Ellises' affluence?" he asked.

She resumed washing dishes. "Hardly. I'd known Conrad since grade school. He was a terror in the classroom but got away with all his antics. He was spoiled and ornery. I don't believe his parents ever said no to him. They indulged him, gave him everything he wanted."

"He wanted you."

She shrugged self-consciously. "He gave every indication that he did. At Mother's urging, I attended a few dances and parties with him. He managed to get close to me at every social, and in that smart-alecky way of his made it understood to everyone that we were a pair. But I didn't like him and was always uneasy whenever we were alone. I think he knew that. I think he enjoyed my unease."

"He still does."

"I'm sure," she murmured. "Anyway, when he failed to woo me, he turned his charm on my mother and formally asked her for my hand. She had dollar signs in her eyes and couldn't see through him. Margaret did. She tried to tell Mother to wake up to his true nature, but she wouldn't listen. When I rejected his proposal, Mother told me that I was a fool and that I would regret my decision."

She rinsed the meat platter and passed it to Mr. Rainwater. Reading the silent question in his expression, she added, "The only thing I regret is that, when she died, she still hadn't forgiven me. She told me I had denied her the one thing that might have made her happy again. She died disappointed and angry with me."

He carried a stack of clean plates to the cabinet and placed them on the shelf. "When did you marry Mr. Barron?"

"Shortly after Mother died. I was running the house then. I'd placed an ad on the bulletin board in the train depot. He worked for the railroad. He saw the ad and came to look at the room. He didn't rent it."

Mr. Rainwater thought that through, then said, "He saw something here he liked better than the room."

"If he'd been living in the house, he couldn't have courted me."

"Did he court you?"

"Quite effectively. He was soft-spoken and polite. I was taken by his manner, which was so different from Conrad's boasting and bullying." Softly she added, "But we both made vows we were unable to keep."

They worked in silence until the last pan was dried and put away. He draped the damp towel over the counter. She drained the sink and the rinse basin. He rolled down his shirtsleeves and fastened his cuff links. She removed her apron and hung it on a hook. He retrieved his jacket and folded it over his arm.

And then both went still.

"Long day," he said.

"Yes. Exhausting."

"As most of your days are."

"I'm used to being tired."

Reluctant to look at him, she leaned across the table and repositioned the salt and pepper shakers in the center of it. The saltshaker tipped over. She righted it. After that, she didn't know what to do with her hands, so after briefly clasping them at her waist, she lowered them to her sides.

"Ella?"

She stared at the floral pattern on the oilcloth covering the table. Grains of salt had spilled onto it, but they blended into the swirl of blue morning glories and red geraniums, so they were almost invisible. Ordinarily she would have swept them into her hand. But now she was afraid to move.

"Ella."

Hearing him speak her given name had made her breath catch, and she was still holding it. She closed her eyes as she exhaled slowly, then raised her head and looked at him.

He said, "I owe you an apology for speaking to you so brusquely this morning."

This morning seemed like a very long time ago. Several moments passed before she recalled the harsh words to which he was referring. I'm *fine*. Spoken in anger from the staircase. "It was nothing."

"I was abrupt and rude. I'm sorry."

"I made a pest of myself."

"You were asking about my health out of genuine concern. That's why I got angry."

She gave her head a slight shake of incomprehension. "Why would my concern make you angry?"

His eyes took on a deeper intensity. "Because you're the last beautiful woman I'll know. When you look at me, I don't want you seeing an invalid."

FOURTEEN

Ella spent a restless night.

Mr. Rainwater didn't come down for breakfast, sending word by Margaret, who'd been upstairs gathering laundry, that he wanted only coffee. Ella sent Margaret back to his room with a tray. When she came downstairs, Ella expected a report on his condition. But Margaret said nothing until she asked.

"He seemed all right to me, Miss Ella."

Ella didn't fish for more, and she resisted the impulse to go and check on him herself. Yesterday she'd pestered him with questions until he'd lost patience with her. She wouldn't make that mistake again, because she didn't want to spark his temper. Nor did she want any more talk of her being beautiful, which she wasn't, or of his wish not to be regarded by her as an invalid. The impropriety of such personal dialogue made her uncomfortable.

Besides, neither her appearance nor how she regarded him

had any relevance to their particular situation, which was that he was a resident in her boardinghouse. Only that. Nothing more.

Nevertheless, she hoped that, if his pain became unbearable, he wouldn't let his masculine pride prevent him from alerting her to it.

After lunch a soft rain began to fall, causing steam to rise off hot surfaces—rooftops, automobiles, railroad tracks. It made the air even heavier with humidity. But the summer shower was a novelty, a rare and wonderful blessing that Ella wanted to enjoy, so she took a sack of string beans with her onto the front porch. She sat in the rocker with the sack of beans and a ceramic bowl in her lap. Solly was beside her on the floor with his bag of empty spools and the box of dominoes.

It was mindless work, breaking the end off the bean pod and pulling away the string that sealed it, then snapping the pod in half or thirds and placing the sections in the bowl. She would cook the beans tomorrow. Maybe she'd toss in some new potatoes with the red jackets still on. It would make a good side dish with baked ham.

Her mind wandered from tomorrow's menu to yesterday's unsettling confrontation with Conrad, to the menace he'd wreaked at the Thompsons' farm last night, and then to the late interlude in the kitchen, where she had barely avoided breaking dishes she'd been washing for watching Mr. Rainwater's hands as he'd dried them.

Ella, he'd said. Twice.

She hadn't acknowledged his addressing her by her first name, because it had been inappropriate, and she hadn't wanted to emphasize the inappropriateness by making it an issue that required further discussion. After his saying what he had about her being beautiful, she'd asked him to excuse her and had beat a hasty retreat to her room.

Still, she had the memory of his speaking her name. Secretly she was glad to have heard the special resonance his voice had lent those two ordinary syllables. Somehow she knew it was a memory she would hold on to for a long time. Possibly forever.

She was so lost in thought that at first she didn't realize Solly was no longer sitting on the painted planks of the porch floor but had got up and moved to the railing.

"Solly?"

He didn't respond, of course. He was intent on standing a domino on its end, directly in line with the post beneath it and squarely in the center of the board that formed the rail. While she'd been woolgathering, he'd been lining up the dominoes, so that now, a dozen formed a straight line along the railing.

She left the sack of beans and the bowl in the seat of her chair and moved closer to the railing, but not so close that she encroached on the boundaries which were invisible to her but crucial to her son. She didn't want her nearness to distract him from what he was doing.

After watching him for several minutes, she saw that he was lining up the dominoes in ascending order. But, more important, he wasn't picking them out of a scattered pile, as he'd done before. He was searching in the box for the next one in sequence before placing it at the end of the line.

This wasn't the uncanny talent that idiot savants frequently displayed, as explained to her by Dr. Kincaid. Apparently Solly possessed that extraordinary trait, too, but today, with the dominoes, he was reasoning. He was thinking it through before choosing the next domino. Essentially, he was counting!

Tears came to her eyes, and she pressed her fingers to her lips to contain a sob of joy.

"Margaret said you didn't have the good sense to come in out of the rain."

She whirled around as Mr. Rainwater pushed open the screened door and stepped onto the porch.

"Look." She pointed at the dominoes on the railing. "He took it upon himself to do this. I didn't begin the project for him. And watch."

Mr. Rainwater came and stood by her side. Solly had added only two dominoes to the row before Mr. Rainwater realized what had caused her excitement. "He's sorting through those in the box until he finds the next one in sequence."

"Don't you think that's significant?"

"Absolutely."

"Sunday, in the cemetery, I remember him gazing at the iron pickets of the gate. Obviously he's intrigued by the ordered and precise placement of things. Couldn't that fascination be fed and nurtured? It could even be developed into a skill, don't you think?"

"I certainly do. He could be building bridges one of these days."

She smiled at his optimism. "I'd be satisfied with much less than that."

Mr. Rainwater reached out and touched Solly's shoulder. The boy flinched, but he didn't stop what he was doing. "Good job, Solly."

"Very good job, Solly," she repeated.

Mr. Rainwater said, "I think this calls for a celebration. An ice cream cone at the very least. Would you let me treat you and Solly?"

"Before dinner?"

"Celebrations should be spontaneous. Rules can be broken—"

"Mr. Rainwater!" Margaret burst through the screened door. Her eyes were wide; she was breathless with alarm. "My boy Jimmy just called from the store, said there's gonna be trouble out the Hatchers' place. Said you need to get there fast. Conrad Ellis and his bunch were in the store talkin' 'bout what they was gonna do to any riffraff that showed up out there tryin' to interfere with gov'ment business."

"I'm leaving now." He brushed past the maid and went inside only long enough to snatch his hat from the hall tree. "Where is the Hatcher place?"

"I'll go with you." Ella took off her apron and tossed it onto the chair.

"Absolutely not," he said. "It could be dangerous."

"It's easier for me to show you to their place than to give directions." Sensing his hesitation, she added, "We're wasting time."

He nodded and charged down the front steps, Ella following.

"Watch Solly, Margaret," she called over her shoulder.

"Don't you worry none 'bout him. You and Mr. Rainwater take care of your ownselves. Jimmy said those peckerwoods was drunk and actin' wild."

By the time they arrived at the beef cattle ranch located several miles west of Gilead, the situation was already tense. Assembled there were Ollie Thompson, Mr. Pritchett, the postmaster, a minister, the shop teacher at the high school, the man who ran the salvage yard, and so many others whom Ella recognized.

They nodded somberly when Mr. Rainwater parked his car and joined them just outside the barbed-wire fence that delineated the pasture. He was the only one of them unarmed.

Standing apart from them was another group, mostly Negroes but some whites. By their gaunt faces and shabby clothing, Ella knew they must have come from shantytown. She recognized the recent widower with the three children, whom Mr. Rainwater had befriended. Standing a full head taller than the others was Brother Calvin, looking grim but calm.

Mr. Rainwater had advised Ella to remain in the car, when actually she had no intention of getting out. The only other woman in sight was Mrs. Hatcher, who was standing in the hardscrabble patch of yard in front of her house, holding on to her husband's arm as though trying to restrain him from doing something reckless.

The rain shower had been short-lived but the cloud cover was thick and oppressive. The air seemed too dense to inhale, made no easier to breathe by the stench of manure from the loaded cattle truck that rumbled through the pasture gate and then down the dirt road in the direction of the main highway.

A wide, deep pit, larger even than the one at the Thompsons' farm, had been gouged out of the pasture. Possibly a hundred head of bawling Angus cattle had been herded into it. Around it, men, with their hats pulled low and rifles aimed, stood awaiting the signal from their leader to start firing.

When they did, Ella jumped.

Even though she was prepared for the barrage, the racket was deafening, assaulting more than the ears. Ella covered hers with her hands, but that only dulled the sound, it didn't mute it. She felt the concussion of each shot against her chest, against her eyelids when she closed her eyes.

The first gunshots had alarmed the cattle. Their lowing of discontent escalated into bellows of terror, heard even above the cacophony of gunfire, which seemed to go on forever. Then there were left only a random few bawling sounds coming from the bottom of the pit. Each was silenced with the clap of a gunshot that echoed off the low-hanging clouds.

The silence that followed was as thick as the gunsmoke that wafted above the carnage.

Ella waited for several seconds, then opened her eyes and lowered her hands from her ears. Her palms were wet with nervous perspiration. She wiped them on her skirt. But none of the men, either in Mr. Rainwater's group or with Brother Calvin, had moved a muscle.

The shooters lowered their rifles and began a slow progress toward the row of black cars, parked fender to fender along the road. A few of them lit smokes. Some entered into mumbled conversations among themselves. All avoided eye contact with the silent spectators.

The leader stopped to say something to Mr. Hatcher. The government man paused, as though waiting for Mr. Hatcher to respond to what he'd said or, by some other means, to acknowledge it. But Mr. Hatcher did nothing except give a brusque motion of his hand. The man moved on and joined the others, who were climbing into the government cars.

No one moved as they drove away.

The convoy had gone several hundred yards, but was still in sight, when Mr. Hatcher called out, "Y'all help yourselves if you like."

Still no one moved. It was Mr. Pritchett who called out, "What did he say to you, Alton?"

"He said they'd be buried sometime today before dark. But not to let y'all butcher any meat off those carcasses or there'd be trouble and weren't nothin' he would do to stop it."

Then Mr. Hatcher turned and crossed his yard to a chopping block that was used for splitting firewood. He grabbed the long handle of an ax and worked the blade out of the heartwood. Shouldering the ax, he walked toward the pit. "He can go to hell. For myself, I ain't gonna deny hungry folks some scraps of stringy beef."

A cheer went up. Brother Calvin gave a signal that seemed to unleash the men with him. They clambered over and under the fence, then ran pell-mell toward the pit, carrying knives, hatchets, and containers for whatever meat they could carve off the bony carcasses. Without a moment's hesitation, they plunged down into the mass grave. Ella realized then what a motivator hunger was.

It wasn't until they had begun hacking at the dead cattle that anyone noticed the roar of engines. She thought perhaps Mr. Rainwater was the first to hear the sound above the gleeful shouting of the shantytown men as they went about their amateur butchering. He was the first to turn toward the sound, and his expression immediately registered alarm.

Ella whipped her head around.

Across the road, speeding out from the cover of dense woods, were several pickup trucks and cars, overflowing with men brandishing firearms and screaming like banshees. They must have been hiding there, motors idling, waiting for this moment.

Their vehicles jounced over the rough ground but didn't slow down. They reached the road going top speed, crossed it, and then braked hard at the edge of the ditch. Men spilled from the vehicles and eddied around Mr. Rainwater's car in a swarm.

Ella saw Mr. Hatcher scramble out of the cattle pit, his

boots fighting for purchase in the moist soil. He ran back to his wife, who seemed petrified by fear. He shooed her into the house and saw to it that the door was locked, then ran back to the rim of the pit, the bloody ax still in his hand.

Brother Calvin admonished the men with him to remain calm and not to do anything foolish. Men from town spread out, taking up positions along the barbed-wire fence, forming a human barricade against the onslaught of the new arrivals.

But all this Ella saw in her peripheral vision, because she was watching Conrad as he stayed behind his vanguard until they were toe-to-toe with the townsmen. Then two of them moved aside and let him saunter between them. He walked straight up to Mr. Rainwater.

Without thinking, Ella opened the car door and got out.

Conrad looked Mr. Rainwater up and down, then turned his head only and made a scoffing sound. His friends laughed. Turning back to Mr. Rainwater, he said, "Are you their ringleader?"

"No."

"Well, whoever your leader is better tell those niggers and ne'er-do-wells to get out of that pit, or they're liable to get buried along with those dead cows."

"Would you shoot unarmed men?"

"They're armed with knives."

"Nobody with a knife has threatened anyone."

"They're breaking the law."

Mr. Rainwater made a show of looking around. "There isn't a lawman here to arrest them."

"The government men put me in charge of making sure no cattle were butchered."

"Do you have documentation of that?"

Conrad hesitated, chewing on the inside of his cheek as he ruminated. "I don't need documentation. I'm in charge."

"So you said," Mr. Rainwater said drily.

"Are you going to get those men out of there, or not?"

"Mr. Ellis, if the government was dead set against these men getting some free beef, Mr. Hatcher's property would be crawling with agents wearing badges. Their sole purpose would be to prevent the field dressing of these cattle."

"Cattle." Conrad spat into the dirt. "They're hide and bones, that's all. Not fit for human consumption."

"Some of the malnourished people in shantytown would beg to differ."

"You sure do use a lot of fancy words."

"Then I'll try to put it more simply. Why would you want to do something so distasteful that even law enforcement agencies avoid it? It's got nothing to do with you, so wouldn't you rather just turn a blind eye? Why don't you and your friends let these men take what meat they can get and carry it back to their hungry families?"

Conrad thrust his face to within an inch of Mr. Rainwater's. "Why don't you kiss my ass?" That won him another round of laughter from his friends, but even that ceased when Conrad drove his fist into Mr. Rainwater's face.

Mr. Rainwater had seen the blow coming and dodged, but not fast enough or far enough. Conrad's knuckles grazed his cheekbone, splitting skin, drawing blood. Mr. Rainwater reeled backward but was saved from landing against the barbed wires by the quick reaction of Tad Wallace, owner of the salvage yard, who put out an arm to catch him.

As soon as he'd steadied Mr. Rainwater, Mr. Wallace lunged

at Conrad. But Mr. Rainwater grabbed him by his shirtsleeve and pulled him back. "That's what he's asking for. An excuse to attack."

Others murmured agreement. Mr. Wallace backed down.

With the back of his hand, Mr. Rainwater swiped at the blood trickling down his face. "You got what you came for, which was a swipe at me. You've made your point. Everybody saw it. They'll talk about it for weeks. You hit me, and now you've got bragging rights. So clear out and leave these folks alone."

Looking amused, Conrad glanced over his shoulder at his buddies, and they all chuckled on cue. "No, we're not ready to clear out just yet. And don't think you and these other yahoos can scare us off with a few shotguns and some rusty knives."

"What about the promise of damnation? Would that scare you?"

No one had noticed that Brother Calvin had climbed out of the pit, circled around, and now was on the outside of the fence, standing behind some of Conrad's gang. His rumbling voice startled them. As he walked forward, they parted. A few of them did so grudgingly, but none impeded him until he stood only a foot away from Conrad. Even he was diminished by Brother Calvin's imposing height and the breadth of his shoulders.

But Conrad wasn't intimidated by the larger man. He sneered at him. "Aren't you the nigger preacher who's been keeping the others agitated?"

"You know who I am. You broke a window of my church, which didn't offend me nearly as much as it offended God. I know you're a bigot, and that doesn't make any difference to me. You'll have to answer for your hatred and prejudices to the Almighty. What matters to me is that people are hungry, and through the generosity and good-heartedness of Mr. Hatcher, here's a chance for them to get some free meat.

"Not just colored people, either. Whites, too. You remember Lansy Roeder?" He motioned toward the pit, where Ella could see the rawboned man in overalls holding a butcher knife in one hand, a basin in the other. His hands, forearms, and clothes were blood-smeared. Lansy hadn't wasted any time trying to get some of the beef before it spoiled.

"Lansy says y'all went to school together," Brother Calvin said to Conrad. "Bank foreclosed on his place three months ago. He and his family were moved out and had nowhere else to go, so they're camping in shantytown. He's picking cotton, but he's making next to nothing. His children are starving."

Conrad remained unmoved. "It's not my fault he can't feed his kids. If he couldn't feed them, why'd he keep having them?" He snickered. "'Course his wife has a real nice shape on her." He looked over his shoulder at his cronies. "Maybe he should put her to work, huh, guys? I know she'd get my business."

His friends roared with bawdy laughter. Several whistled. Lansy dropped his basin and charged forward. Knowing he wouldn't stand a chance against Conrad, two men wrestled him to the ground and held him there while he shouted invectives. This indignity made Conrad's group laugh all the more.

But when Conrad came back around to Brother Calvin, he wasn't laughing, or even smiling. "I'm giving you one minute to get away from here, or we're going to start shooting. And I'm not bullshitting you, preacher."

Mr. Rainwater stepped forward. "You'll have to shoot past us."

Conrad extended his hand behind him, and one of his friends slapped a pistol into his palm. He aimed it at Mr. Rainwater's middle. "Fine by me. I'll start with you, Mr. Fancy Words."

Ella's blood froze in her veins. There was a nervous shifting among Mr. Rainwater's allies. They'd left their lunches uneaten, closed their shops, hurried from their homes, to rush to the aid of their neighbors. Now, they were threatened with becoming victims of the violence they'd hoped to prevent. The reality of a standoff against armed men was much more daunting than the prospect had seemed during their covert meetings.

In contrast to them, Mr. Rainwater remained unflappable. "I didn't think you were that stupid, Mr. Ellis."

Conrad made a jabbing motion with the pistol.

Mr. Rainwater didn't flinch. "I didn't think you would be stupid enough to gun down men in cold blood when there are so many witnesses."

"I'll take my chances."

"Yes, I'm sure you would. Since you've got Sheriff Anderson in your pocket." Mr. Rainwater angled his head to one side. "Who do you know at the FBI?"

Conrad blinked. "The FBI?"

"The Federal Bureau of—"

"I know what FBI stands for. This isn't their business."

"It will be. You said the government men put you in charge. Which I doubt. But if that's true, and a bunch of people wind up dead or seriously injured, who do you think is going to be left holding the bag? The marksmen, who were just doing their job? People from DRS? Bureaucrats?" He snuffled and shook his head. "If this turns into a bloodbath, they—from President Roosevelt on down—are going to blame you for shedding a bad light on a government program that's meant to help people. But I guess you want a fight so bad, none of that matters to you."

One of Conrad's cronies stepped up behind him and whispered something in his ear. Ella couldn't hear what he said, but it didn't set well. "Shut up," Conrad barked and, as though swatting at a housefly, motioned him back. To Mr. Rainwater, he said, "You think you're smart, don't you?"

"I think you are, Mr. Ellis. I think you're too smart to continue this."

"Come on, Conrad," one of his friends whined.

"Yeah, let's get outta here."

"Let 'em have the goddamn cows. Who cares?"

"Let's go get drunk."

Muttering among themselves, they lowered their weapons and began shuffling away, slowly returning to their pickups and cars.

Eventually, Conrad was the only one left facing the line of resolute townsmen.

He took a few steps backward, then he pointed his pistol at all the men in turn, wagging it like a shaking finger. "Y'all know me, and you know I mean what I say. This isn't over. Not by a long shot." Then he fired the revolver into the air until all six chambers were empty. Only then did he turn and stalk away.

Ella still stood in the wedge of the open car door. Fury blazed from Conrad's eyes as he stormed past her, snarling, "You chose wrong again, Ella."

FIFTEEN

"Isn't Mr. Rainwater joining us tonight?" Miss Violet asked as Ella served the sisters their salads.

"He's out with friends."

"Oh." Miss Pearl couldn't mask her disappointment. She was wearing a fresh flower in her hair.

Miss Violet sighed. "And Mr. Hastings is gone again, so it's just the two of us tonight, Sister."

Trying to inject a bright note, Ella said, "You'll have both parlors all to yourselves."

Not even the promise of that elevated their mood. They ate their meal as mechanically as Ella served it. Her mind was elsewhere, with Mr. Rainwater and the others who'd stayed behind to carve what edible meat they could from the slaughtered cattle and distribute it among those living in shantytown and to any other area families whose situations were dire.

"It's nasty work," Mr. Rainwater had told her after insisting he drive her back to town.

"I'm not afraid of raw meat. I could help."

"You have other responsibilities."

He was right, of course. But after having won the standoff against Conrad, she felt a bit let down to be returning to the mundane chore of preparing and serving dinner to her elderly boarders.

"And I don't trust Conrad's surrender," Mr. Rainwater had said, adding it as a footnote. "He may come back. There may still be trouble."

Ella feared Mr. Rainwater was right about that, too. After being publicly humiliated, the Conrad she knew would be plotting a harsh reprisal.

Then Mr. Rainwater had asked, "What did he say to you as he left?"

"Something about me being on the wrong side." She had remembered word-for-word Conrad's parting shot, but the paraphrase omitted the personal connotation, which she'd rather not share with Mr. Rainwater.

He had dropped her at home, apologizing for not walking her to the door. "I need to get back to Hatcher's place right away. I probably won't be back by dinnertime."

"Take care."

He'd touched the brim of his hat and driven away, looking like a man who'd won his first battle and was returning to the front, flush with excitement over his victory and eager to experience more of it.

By nature, Ella wasn't a fighter and avoided confrontation whenever possible. All the same, she envied Mr. Rainwater's—indeed, any man's—freedom to return to the fray and have his mettle tested.

After the sisters finished their dinner and went into the parlor to play cards, Ella coaxed Solly into eating. Margaret looked on, bragging on each bite he took. The maid was in good spirits tonight, having heard from Ella the outcome of the showdown. She'd extolled the courage of Brother Calvin, Mr. Rainwater, and the other men for standing up to Conrad, saying it was "'bout time that bully got his comeuppance."

Ella doubted they'd heard the last of Conrad, but she kept her misgivings to herself.

While Margaret finished the dishes, Ella put Solly down for the night and said good night to the spinsters as they made their way upstairs, arguing over the score of their gin game.

Margaret intended to stop in shantytown before going home. Ella sent her off with two baskets of leftovers, then ate her own dinner alone at the kitchen table. Just as she was finishing, she heard a car. She made her way quickly to the front door and tried not to reveal her disappointment when she saw Dr. Kincaid huffing up the steps onto the porch.

"Good evening, Mrs. Barron," he said when he saw her through the screen. "I hoped to catch you before you went to bed."

She unlatched the door. "My bedtime will be a while yet. Come in."

As soon as he was inside, she motioned him toward the formal parlor. "Would you like a glass of tea?"

"No thank you. I just finished dinner. Is David here?"

"He's out tonight."

"Hmm." He removed his hat and took a seat. "I received this today and wanted to share it with you as soon as possible."

He extended to her a large envelope. It had been opened.

Ella sat down and withdrew several typewritten sheets clipped together. She read the letterhead, scanned the top sheet, then looked at the doctor expectantly.

"He's a well-respected specialist," he explained. "He's conducted several studies. I told you I'd written to doctors around the country, asking for information about idiot savants. One of them remembered my request and was kind enough to send this to me. The article was published several months ago in a medical journal. I thought you'd find it interesting and encouraging. I did."

"Thank you." She flipped through the pages, reading the paragraph headings which had been underlined.

"Some of the children with developmental impairments similar to Solly's are being taught to speak and read with comprehension, quite effectively in some instances," Dr. Kincaid said. "Of course, no one, not even this world-renowned specialist, can boast one hundred percent success, but any measurable improvement is a stupendous step forward, wouldn't you say?"

She held the sheets against her chest, crossing her hands over them as though clutching a treasure. "Thank you, Dr. Kincaid. You can't know how grateful I am for your interest."

"I believe I do," he said, smiling.

She told him about Solly's achievement that day. "He's only putting dominoes in a line and in numerical order, but I doubt most children his age would have the concentration or the attention span to be that . . . um . . ."

"Meticulous?"

"Yes."

"So says the doctor in his paper," he said, nodding toward the sheets she still clutched. "That preciseness is a common trait among children with Solly's symptoms. After reading about this study, I believe I was wrong to urge you to keep him medicated. No one actually knows the mental capacity of savants, and that capacity no doubt varies from patient to patient. Solly can't communicate the level of his intelligence, so we have no way of knowing what his capabilities are. He may be limited to lining up dominoes, or he may harbor a brilliant mind. In any case, you owe it to him and to yourself to make that determination if it's at all possible to do so."

She told him she'd written to several schools. "I haven't received any replies yet, so I don't know what will come of my inquiries. These particular institutions may have no experience with children like Solly. If they do have suitable curriculums, the expense of enrolling him would probably be prohibitive." She paused, then added quietly, "Besides, I can't imagine sending him away."

"Even if it was the best thing you could do for him?"

"He may not qualify, Dr. Kincaid. The choice may not be mine to make."

"But if it does come down to being your choice . . ."

Unprepared to commit, she murmured, "We'll see."

After a moment, he slapped his hands on his thighs and stood up. "I should run along. Mrs. Kincaid is silly about going to bed before I get home."

Ella showed him to the door and profusely thanked him again for bringing her the research paper. "I can't wait to read it thoroughly."

"I think you'll find it enlightening. After you've had time to digest the information, let's talk again."

"Certainly."

His gaze moved to the upper floor, then came back to her. "How's he doing?"

She knew he was no longer speaking of Solly. "He got snippy

with me yesterday. He'd told me repeatedly that he was feeling fine, but I continued to badger him. He finally had enough." That was essentially the truth. The doctor didn't need to know the details of why her hovering had nettled Mr. Rainwater. "Ordinarily he's so even-tempered."

"He can also be bullheaded. He was the most stubborn child I've ever run across. Not bratty, just persistent. Once he set his mind to something, he would wear you down until he got his way." He chuckled. "I also remember him pitching a temper tantrum or two when he didn't."

She couldn't envision Mr. Rainwater throwing a tantrum, but she could imagine him being mulish. Twice, his steely resolve had forced Conrad to stand down.

Dr. Kincaid frowned. "You said he was out."

She nodded.

"I suppose he was at Alton Hatcher's ranch today. And in shantytown tonight."

Again she nodded.

"I tried to discourage his involvement in this business. You don't want Conrad Ellis and his gang as enemies."

"I tried to tell him that, too, Dr. Kincaid. It did no good."

The doctor sighed. "It wouldn't."

"Has he always been committed to causes like this?"

"Lost causes you mean?"

"Why do you say it's a lost cause?"

"Because throughout history there have been bullies, and I don't think that's likely to change. During this economic depression there are going to be those who suffer, and vultures who take advantage of their suffering. Others, angry over the situation, will take out their anger on blameless people, committing theft, assault, even murder in increased numbers. But, just so I don't sound like an old codger, a prophet of doom and gloom, let me add that hard times can also bring out the best in people."

"Like Mr. Rainwater."

"The answer to your earlier question is yes. David typically takes up for the underdog. I think he grew up feeling guilty for the advantages he was born with."

She would never have asked what those advantages entailed but was glad when Dr. Kincaid volunteered them.

"David's father inherited thousands of acres of good land, and he was a savvy cotton grower. He made a lot of money during the Great War. David learned the business, literally from the ground up, and he was a quick study. By the time he was an adolescent, he knew more about cotton growing and marketing than most men who'd been in the business for decades.

"Dutifully he went to college and learned even more about business. Upon graduation he became a successful broker in his own right. He got top dollar for his cotton, and smaller farmers trusted him to get the best possible price for their crops, too. He did well, and he still owns the acreage that made his daddy rich. The market is so low now, he only cultivates a fraction of it, but he hasn't cast off a single tenant. The yield and income from it is substantially less than it's been in years past, but when this depression is over . . . well, the land isn't going anywhere, and there will always be a market for cotton."

What he was telling her, without coming right out and saying so, was that David Rainwater had significant money. "He could live anywhere. Why here?" she asked.

"For one thing, he wanted me to treat him. Don't ask me why. I guess that once he'd received the diagnosis and was told he was terminal, he wanted to be near family. Mrs. Kincaid and I are his only family."

"He never married?"

"No, but not for lack of opportunity," he said, laughing softly. "Every single lady in North Texas tried to nab him. David's an attractive man, but I imagine there were gold diggers among his admirers. He suspected that, too. I asked him once why he remained a bachelor when he had lovely ladies throwing themselves at him. He told me he was holding out for a woman who wanted him for himself, not for his means."

Thoughtfully he tugged on his earlobe. "A wife could be of great comfort to him now. I wonder if he laments his decision to remain single." Then he shook his head. "If I know David, he doesn't. He's not one to look back with regret."

Ella was still curious as to why Mr. Rainwater, who apparently could afford better, would opt to live in a boardinghouse. "He could be in a house of his own," she mused aloud. "One much grander than mine."

"He had a house of his own. He left it and came here. I suppose he'd rather not be alone while going through this. I think he much prefers the family atmosphere to solitude." He looked at her for a long moment, then put on his hat. "I really must say good night. Let me know what you think of the research paper. It goes without saying to call me if David takes a downturn."

"Of course. Good night. Thank you again."

After seeing him off, she went back into the parlor, took a seat near the brightest lamp, and began to read the medical report. She was going through it a second time when Mr. Rainwater returned.

She was at the door before he reached it. When she saw him, her heart surged to her throat and she gasped.

"It's all right," he said quickly. "It isn't my blood."

"Good Lord."

"I told you it was messy business. I can't come into your house like this. Do you mind if I go around back, use the faucet in the laundry shed to wash up?"

"I'll bring a bar of soap and a towel to the back door."

"Could I also trouble you to fetch me some clean clothes?"

"I'll bring them right down."

He descended the front steps, then disappeared around the corner of the house. Ella hurried upstairs to his room. She found shirts and slacks hanging neatly in the closet, and hesitated only a moment before opening his bureau drawer and taking out a pair of undershorts and a pair of socks.

She had touched his undergarments before, when she and Margaret did laundry. But they always left their boarders' clothes folded on the bed. It was disturbingly different to take such personal items from his bureau drawer.

From the bathroom, she got a cloth, towel, and bar of soap, then hastened downstairs, through the kitchen, to the back door, where he was waiting. She pushed open the screened door. He reached for the items, but she withheld them. "If you touch the clothes, they'll only get blood on them. I'll carry them out for you."

"Thank you."

She picked her way across the dark backyard to the shed and set his clothes and the articles from the bathroom on the worktable where she kept detergent and bleach. "There's no light out here."

"I'll manage."

"Are you hungry?"

"Not for red meat."

She smiled at his wryness. "I made chicken salad for tomorrow's lunch."

"I'm troubling you already."

"I'll fix you a sandwich." She left him. Before she entered the house, she heard the squeal of the faucet being turned on and the splash of water.

She made the sandwich, then put it on a plate along with sliced tomatoes and a wedge of cantaloupe. She also cut a piece of pound cake and put it on a separate plate. Not knowing what he would want to drink, she put an empty glass at the place setting and fixed a pot of coffee, leaving it on the stove ready to brew if he asked for it.

Then she sat down, her back to the door, and waited.

When she heard him pull open the screened door, she turned. He was standing on one leg, pulling on his sock. "My shoes are filthy. I'll have to clean them in the morning, when I can see better." He switched legs and pulled on his other sock, then walked into the kitchen.

He smelled of soap. His hair was wet, finger-combed back off his face. "I left my clothes soaking in a washtub. I hope that's all right."

"Margaret will see to them in the morning."

"I can't ask her to do that."

She motioned him toward the table, where his supper was waiting. "She'll do it gladly. Since she heard about your face-off with Conrad, you're her hero."

He looked at the food. "I didn't think I was hungry, but this looks awfully good. Thanks."

"I can get a tray if you'd rather eat in your room."

"Here's fine." He pulled the chair from beneath the table and sat down.

"What would you like to drink?"

"Milk, please."

She filled the glass beside his plate, but after replacing the milk bottle in the icebox, she was unsure what to do next, leave him to eat alone, or join him at the table?

He looked up, his mouth full. He swallowed. "What's the matter?"

"Do you want company?"

He slid his chair back and stood up. "Mrs. Barron?" He indicated the chair across the table from him. "Please."

She frowned at the formality but sat down. "I thought you might be tired of talking about it."

"I'm tired, but in a good way."

"So it went well? No more trouble?"

"No more trouble. No sign of Conrad Ellis or any of his band. We managed to butcher several head before the front loaders showed up to bury them. The rest of the time was spent distributing the meat so it could be cooked before it spoiled. The man who owns the ice company?"

"Mr. Miller."

"He was generous enough to donate several blocks of ice to pack some of the meat in until we could get it distributed."

"Dr. Kincaid said these times would bring out the best in people."

"When did you see him?"

She told him about the doctor's visit and the article on the study that he'd left with her. His eyes shone with interest. "When you're finished, I'd like to read it if I may."

"I'll welcome your opinion."

He finished his meal and stood up. "I'll be right back."

He was out of the kitchen before she could ask where he

was going. She washed his dishes and upturned them on the counter to dry. She was just about to turn out the lights when he reappeared, bringing with him a book.

He grinned as he extended it to her. "Seems everyone is bringing you reading material today."

Ella took the book from him and read the title. *A Farewell to Arms*. "You finished it?"

"This morning. That's why I didn't come down for breakfast. I didn't want to stop until I'd read it through. I was going to give it to you immediately, but then the day got away from us."

She ran her fingertips over the lettering spelling out the title. "I'll read it as quickly as I can and get it back to you. In the meantime, I'll take excellent care of it."

"It's a gift, Ella."

Quickly she looked up at him. "I can't accept it."

"Please do. Please. I want you to have it."

She held his gaze for as long as she could stand the intensity of it, then lowered her head and stared at the book cover. "Is the ending sad?"

"Very."

Ella felt the heat of his gaze on the crown of her head. She felt the pressure of the walls, which seemed to be closing in, and the weight of air against her skin where it was exposed. Her throat became painfully tight.

In a low voice he said, "Even knowing the ending was sad, I wouldn't have deprived myself the beauty of the story. Would you?"

She glanced up, but looking into his face caused her heart to swell, so she dropped her gaze back to the book. She couldn't answer. She didn't *know* her answer. She sought it in the words on the book cover, but they began to blur.

She was looking at them through tears.

Sixteen

The following day, she avoided him.

He came down for breakfast and chatted cheerfully with the Dunne sisters, who pestered him with questions about his rare evening out. They were curious to know how he'd spent it and with whom. As Ella moved in and out of the dining room, she didn't hear all his replies, but he soon had steered the conversation to the ladies' favorite radio programs.

Each time he tried to catch Ella's eye, she avoided looking at him. Two nights in a row, he'd been the last person to whom she'd said good night, and that was unsettling. Although their conversations had touched on personal subjects, nothing improper had happened between them.

But she would be less than honest with herself if she didn't admit that their relationship had shifted to something beyond that of landlady and boarder. There had been an air of intimacy during those moments. She wouldn't have been the least troubled had she had a one-on-one conversation with Mr. Hastings. In fact, there had been times when he returned from a trip too late to have dinner in the dining room, so she had served him a cold supper in the kitchen. She hadn't felt any self-consciousness last night sitting alone with Dr. Kincaid in the parlor.

But being alone with Mr. Rainwater was different.

With him she felt uncertain and flustered. It was nothing he said or did that made her feel this way. He never touched her. Well, only her hand, and only once. There were no salacious overtones in his conversation, even in his remark about her being a beautiful woman. She couldn't fault his comportment.

It was his mere presence that caused an unaccountable tension in her chest. Last night, being close enough to feel his breath on her face, and hearing the bittersweet sadness in his voice, had provoked tears. When they spilled from her eyes onto her cheeks, she had wished him a good night and fled, just as she had the night before. But last night she'd feared she hadn't made her getaway fast enough. He had seen her tears and would have wondered what had caused them. *She* had wondered.

Something about his insisting that she accept the sentimental novel as a gift had caused an outpouring of emotions, when ordinarily she held them firmly intact. Having had years of practice, she was skilled at containing fear, anger, heartache, even joy. She was certainly adept at holding back tears. But in the quiet of her kitchen, interrupted only by the ticking of the clock and the thrum of her own heartbeat, her rigid control had deserted her.

It frightened her, this loss of restraint. She didn't want to feel any emotion that keenly, believing that if she ever allowed any slippage in the wall of protection she'd built around her heart, she wouldn't be able to prevent its total collapse. And then where would she be?

Exactly where she was now. Her circumstances wouldn't have changed. She would still be living as a widow without benefit of the official status. Her child would still be locked inside a realm she couldn't trespass. Day would follow day, each exactly the same, all with their endless, thankless chores, without any relief or respite or even a sense of accomplishment after having done them.

But if she ever gave way to self-pity, she would be reduced by it, made weaker by it, and left even more susceptible to disappointment and despair.

That's what she'd tried to explain to Mr. Rainwater when she stopped him from weeding the vegetable garden. She had her life in careful but precarious balance, and she couldn't allow anything or anyone to upset it.

But what she feared most, what had kept her tossing and turning sleeplessly last night, was the fear that the scales already had been tipped, and that it was too late to set them aright.

Today, her fear manifested itself in a cross mood that Margaret remarked upon as she prepared the string beans to simmer. After Ella admonished her for the second time to go easy on the bacon grease, she muttered, "Somebody's got they's jaw out of joint this mornin'."

Ignoring her, Ella went about doing her routine tasks, even invented extra ones, to more easily avoid Mr. Rainwater. Which she did successfully until after dinner, when he came out onto the porch, where she was sitting in a rocking chair, watching Solly as he lined up the dominoes along the rail.

Mr. Rainwater let the screened door close gently behind him as he joined them. "He's at it again?"

"Of his own accord. I brought the dominoes out. He took the box from me and went to work." Even her determination to keep her distance from Mr. Rainwater couldn't dampen her pride in this small achievement or her optimism for Solly's future.

"Thank you for leaving the medical report in my room. I read it this afternoon. I understand why you're excited about this study."

"I wish there were a way for that specialist to see Solly. There isn't, of course, but I'm thinking of asking Dr. Kincaid to write to him, describing Solly's characteristics and behavior. Since his paper was published, I'm sure he's been overwhelmed with inquiries from parents as desperate as I am. But he may be more inclined to reply to another physician than to an anxious mother."

"I'm sure Murdy would do that for you."

In silence they watched until Solly had lined up all the dominoes, then Mr. Rainwater said, "Good job, Solly."

Ella said, "Yes, Solly. Good job."

"We were stopped from celebrating yesterday." Mr. Rainwater took out his pocket watch and checked the time. "The drugstore is open until nine-thirty. Let's go to town and get an ice cream cone."

"It's too late."

"It's a celebration."

"The last time I tried feeding Solly an ice cream cone, he got upset when it began to melt over his hand. He didn't like the mess."

"Then we'll get his in a cup."

"Thank you, Mr. Rainwater, but it's time I put him to bed."

"Miss Ella?"

"Out here, Margaret."

Margaret came onto the porch, wearing her hat, her handbag on her arm. "I's leavin' 'less you need me to do something else before I go."

"Thank you, no. I'll see you in the morning."

Mr. Rainwater said, "I'm trying to talk Mrs. Barron into letting me take her and Solly to the drugstore for some ice cream. Maybe she'll agree to it if you come with us. I'll drive you home after."

"I can't sit at the soda fountain, Mr. Rainwater. You know that."

"I don't want to sit at the soda fountain," he said. "I was thinking of taking a stroll around the square while I was eating my cone."

"It's too late to go downtown," Ella said, but neither of them paid her attention.

Margaret was beaming a smile at Mr. Rainwater. "I'm partial to plain ol' vanilla."

"My favorite is strawberry. How about you, Mrs. Barron?"

"Chocolate. But it's too late—"

"Come on, Miss Ella," Margaret wheedled. "It's just now twenty minutes past dark, and it's pleasant out. How come you won't let Mr. Rainwater buy Solly an ice cream?"

He had outfoxed her. There was no way she could refuse without denying Margaret a treat, because he couldn't be seen strolling around the square alone with a colored lady without inviting censure from both whites and Negroes.

Defeated and, actually, not all that unhappy about it, Ella said, "I'll get my hat."

Ella had resolved not to be seen riding with him again. If people saw them often together in his car, they would begin to talk. But there weren't too many people on the streets of town this evening. The square was deserted when he parked in front of the drugstore.

The only person she had to worry about gossiping was Doralee, Mr. Gerald's plain and thus far unmarried daughter, who was tending the fountain tonight. She was terribly bucktoothed and compensated for it with a sour disposition, being ugly to people before they had a chance to be ugly to her, Ella supposed.

Doralee was squinting at them curiously through the store's windows as they climbed out of Mr. Rainwater's car and approached the door. Ella said, "Solly and I will wait out here with Margaret."

"What flavor will Solly want?"

Remembering the screeching fit he'd pitched when the melting ice cream had dripped over his hands, she said, "Vanilla." Any mess made with vanilla would be easier to clean up.

"Chocolate for you?"

"Please."

"Looks like Brother Calvin is working late," Margaret remarked as she sat down beside Ella on the bench outside the store.

Ella followed her gaze toward the AME church. It was two blocks off the town square, on Elm Street, which was the racial demarcation of town. Because the lights were on inside, the church was visible through the trees even at this distance.

"I guess he's fixin' that broke window," Margaret mused. "We took up a love offering for it on Sunday."

Mr. Rainwater paused on his way into the drugstore. "Go and invite him to join us."

Margaret smiled at him. "That's very kindly of you, Mr. Rainwater."

Margaret left the bench and stepped into the street. She

crossed it, then walked along the sidewalk to the nearest corner, where she turned out of sight.

Ella could hear Mr. Rainwater ordering their ice creams, adding one for the minister. "And put one of those vanillas in a cup, please. We're going to walk around the square, but I'll bring your cup back, I promise."

"I trust you, Mr. Rainwater."

Absently Ella wondered how he'd managed to disarm even the prickly Doralee Gerald, who had addressed him by name in a simpering tone reminiscent of that of Miss Pearl, whom Ella had asked to latch the screened door behind them as they left the house.

Miss Pearl seemed perturbed that they were leaving her and her sister alone in the house and had asked how long they planned on being gone. Ella had told her not long, resenting having to account for her time to someone who paid her rent.

Beside her on the bench, Solly was staring straight ahead, rocking back and forth, tapping the toes of his shoes together, unmindful of the mosquito that lighted on his knee. Ella brushed it away. Solly continued to rock.

A lean and hungry-looking dog trotted down the center of the street, and Ella, not recognizing it, tensed, but it went past without giving them a glance.

In the next block, she noticed a light going off in an office building. Moments later the town's only lawyer and his secretary came out of the office. He locked the door behind them, then together they got into his car and drove away. His wife had been an invalid for ten years. Rumors had circulated about the nature of his relationship with the young, pretty secretary.

"Here we are." Mr. Rainwater pushed his way through the door, carrying a clear glass dish of ice cream for Solly and a chocolate cone for her. "Miss Doralee is dishing up—"

He was interrupted by a scream so piercing that even Solly reacted. He stopped rocking, stopped tapping his toes together.

Ella shot to her feet.

Mr. Rainwater dropped the dish and the cone he was carrying onto the sidewalk and bolted across the street, running in the direction of the AME church, from where the scream seemed to have come. He didn't go to the corner but plunged into the alley between the grocery store and the post office.

Another scream rent the night air.

Ella grabbed Solly's hand and followed Mr. Rainwater. When she and Solly reached the other side of the street, she was practically dragging her son as she ran into the shadows of the alley into which Mr. Rainwater had disappeared. It opened into a wider alley, which ran the length of the block behind the commercial buildings.

The lane was pocked with deep ruts. It was littered with debris, an attraction for rats, tomcats, and other nocturnal scavengers. Two men were running down the center of the alley, their backs to her. One knocked over a trash barrel, but he didn't stop.

In the fence that bordered the alley, she noticed that several of the boards were missing, creating an opening. Gripping Solly's hand, she squeezed him with her between the slats, wondering if Mr. Rainwater had created that opening when he passed through only moments ahead of her.

On the other side of the fence was the backyard of an abandoned house that looked even more neglected and derelict in the darkness. Without decreasing her speed, she forged a path through the weeds and across the uneven ground, her heart in her throat and her lungs already burning with exertion.

A car was coming down Oak Street. She and Solly ran through the twin beams of its headlights as they crossed that street. She heard the squeal of brakes, but she didn't stop to apologize to the startled driver.

She had gained on Mr. Rainwater. He was still running, but he seemed to have a stitch in his side. He had a hand to it as he crossed Elm Street and entered the churchyard. Ella was only steps behind him by the time he climbed the stairs to the door of the church. Inside, the screams had been reduced to keening.

Before going in, he glanced back at Ella. "Don't look."

His warning came too late. Through the open door, she saw Brother Calvin hanging by his neck from a ceiling beam.

Margaret was inconsolable.

Mr. Rainwater drew her up from her huddled position and guided her across the threshold onto the stairs. Ella sat down beside her on the top step and embraced her, murmuring words of comfort that she knew were banal and useless.

Mr. Rainwater and she had been the first to reach the church, but others, alerted by Margaret's screams, converged from every direction of the colored community. Mr. Rainwater had closed the church door, but the hanging body could easily be seen through the windows. Cries of horror and outrage punctuated the low buzz of hushed voices. There was weeping. Children, who ordinarily would have been running about and chasing lightning bugs, were standing wide-eyed and subdued, staring at the lighted sanctuary. The dog that Ella had seen earlier was barking ferociously.

A car stopped at the curb, and the lawyer Ella had seen leaving his office minutes before got out. He hung back, obviously concerned but not to the point of wanting to become involved. Then he spied Ella.

Reluctantly, he threaded his way through the crowd. Approaching the church stairs, he removed his hat. "Mrs. Barron? Miss Lillian and I heard screams. I almost hit you and your boy with my car."

"The pastor has been lynched, Mr. Whitehead."

"Oh." He released the word on a sigh of deep regret and sympathy, making Ella feel sorry for all the times she'd given even a thought to the gossip about him and his secretary.

"Could you notify the sheriff, please?" Mr. Rainwater asked.

The lawyer looked beyond Ella at him and must have sensed his trait of calm command. "Right away, sir." He replaced his hat and ran back to his car, where his secretary anxiously waited.

Mr. Rainwater knelt down beside Ella. His face was damp with sweat, and he looked pale. She remembered him holding his side and running with an uneven gait. "Are you in pain?"

He shook his head. "Just winded. Here is the key to my car." He opened her hand and pressed the key into it. "I'll wait for the sheriff. Take Margaret home. You can come back by here and pick me up."

"Won't he need her to tell him what she saw? For his investigation."

His lips formed a thin line. "There won't be an investigation."

Ella arrived at Margaret's house, surprised to find a gathering of her friends and relatives. Although she shouldn't have been surprised. Word of something this tragic had a way of spreading quickly.

Men stood in the yard, smoking and talking among themselves. Children, too young to understand what had taken place, were sleeping on pallets that had been spread on the porch. One elderly woman with a corncob pipe clamped in the corner of her toothless mouth was fanning the sleeping children with a newspaper.

Other women were waiting inside the house for Margaret's return. Ella left Solly in the front seat of the car, where he seemed content, and helped Margaret alight. The men removed their hats and stood aside respectfully as Ella guided Margaret up onto the porch. Margaret's son, Jimmy, in whom she thought the sun rose and set, was waiting just inside the door. As soon as they cleared it, Margaret let out a wail of grief and collapsed into his arms. They were then surrounded by the women who'd come to render aid and share her sorrow.

Knowing that Margaret would be well taken care of, Ella turned to go. As she stepped out onto the porch, Jimmy followed her. "Thank you, Miz Barron," he said.

"This is terrible for her, Jimmy. She thought so highly of Brother Calvin. We all did."

"Yes, ma'am." He looked across the yard for a moment, then his eyes came back to her. "We all know who did it."

The young man looked more angry than mournful, and his anger made Ella afraid for him. She looked at him with appeal. "Don't make trouble for yourself, Jimmy. Your mother would never recover if something happened to you."

"I'll be careful."

That wasn't exactly a promise not to seek reprisal for the lynching, but Ella knew it wasn't her place to admonish him. "Tell Margaret not to come back to work until she feels up to it."

"I will."

"And let me know when the funeral is."

"Thank you again for bringing her home." Then he looked at her with puzzlement. "How come y'all were in town tonight?"

She told him about Mr. Rainwater taking them to get ice cream and sending Margaret to invite Brother Calvin to join them. Jimmy lowered his head, and when, after a moment, he raised it, she saw tears standing in his eyes. He thanked her again, then turned and went back into the house.

"He seemed very touched by your kindness to his mother," Ella told Mr. Rainwater, concluding her account to him of what had happened when she took Margaret home. "It was amazing to me that so many people already knew about the lynching and had gathered at her house."

Only a few people were still at the AME church when she returned to pick him up. The sheriff's car was parked in front. He was talking to the justice of the peace, who'd been summoned to pronounce Brother Calvin dead. A few curious onlookers were milling about.

Mr. Rainwater was standing apart from everyone else, near the street. He got into the car as soon as Ella brought it to a stop, leaving her to drive. Now, he glanced down at Solly, who was sitting between them docilely. "He looks almost asleep."

"He ran along beside me all the way from the drugstore to the church. Through it all, he's been a real trouper. I couldn't have asked for him to behave any better."

"Maybe he sensed you needed him to."

"Maybe."

Solly was asleep by the time they arrived at the house. Ella welcomed the sweet pressure of his head against her arm and almost hated having to get out. "I'll get him," Mr. Rainwater said.

Gently he lifted Solly into his arms, being careful not to awaken him.

Both Dunne sisters rushed to the front door to let them in. They were dressed in nightclothes, slippers, and hairnets. They were twittering, speaking over each other.

"We've been scared out of our wits!" Miss Pearl exclaimed.

"What's going on in town? We heard sirens."

"Mr. Rainwater, you look peaked."

Ella looked at him. As Miss Violet had observed, he did look peaked.

"What's the matter with the boy?"

"Nothing, Miss Pearl. He's only sleeping. And I'm fine, just a bit winded." Mr. Rainwater carried Solly past them in the direction of Ella's room.

She followed him, saying over her shoulder, "You can go to bed. There was a . . . a situation on the other side of town tonight. Sheriff Anderson was summoned. Everything is fine now." Soon enough they would learn of the lynching and Margaret's unwitting involvement, but Ella didn't want to go into it with them tonight. "I'm sorry you had to stay up later than usual to let us in."

"We couldn't have slept anyway with God knows what all going on in colored town."

Ella bit back an angry retort. They were old. Their attitude was wrong and ignorant, but hopelessly ingrained. "Good night, ladies. I'll see you at breakfast." She left them at the foot of the staircase and continued on toward her room.

Mr. Rainwater was standing in the center of it, holding Solly in his arms. "Through there." Ella pointed him toward the small room in which Solly slept. He squeezed through the narrow doorway and laid Solly carefully on the bed. She slipped off Solly's shoes but decided to forgo pajamas tonight and let him sleep in his clothes. "Thank you, Mr. Rainwater."

"Will you join me on the porch?"

"I don't think so. It's late."

"Please? There's something I need to tell you."

SEVENTEEN

"Conrad Ellis has been deputized."

Mr. Rainwater broke that to her the moment she joined him on the porch, before she had even sat down.

"*What?*"

"I'm afraid you heard me right. The sheriff made him a deputy. At his request, I'm sure."

Stunned by this news, she moved to the railing where Solly's dominoes had been left standing in their precise row. "How do you know?"

"He arrived with the sheriff, sporting a badge, carrying a shotgun. He made certain I saw both. He had the honor of being appointed to cut down Brother Calvin."

"From the beam on which he'd hanged him."

"Almost certainly."

She turned, and they stared at each other across the distance separating them. But the enormous inequity of the situation had left Ella speechless. Apparently Mr. Rainwater had nothing to say, either. He looked dispirited and tired. His face was gaunt. She noticed that, when he stood up, he was holding his side. He walked to the door, pulled open the screened door, then looked back at her.

"I don't need to tell you what this means."

"Conrad has been given authority to run roughshod over anyone he chooses and to get away with it."

"You must take care."

"And so must you."

Mr. Rainwater nodded, then went inside.

Ella picked the dominoes off the railing one by one and stacked them neatly inside their box. Solly would appreciate her orderliness. She smiled at the thought.

But, in spite of her smile, an unheralded sob escaped her. She secured the lid on the box of dominoes and clasped it to her chest as though it were a lifeline in a sea of sorrow.

Tears formed, then flowed. She covered her mouth with one hand in an effort to suppress the sobs, but they wouldn't be contained. She cried for Margaret, who'd had the misfortune of making that ghastly discovery. She cried for Brother Calvin, who'd been kind, generous, idealistic, and courageous. While she admired him for standing up to Conrad, and warning him of damnation, she knew he'd died because of his outspokenness. And what of his young wife? Did she know that bigotry had made her a widow?

She wept for Jimmy, who, because of this incident, would become embittered and angry, filled with hatred and a thirst for revenge. For Ollie and Lola. For the Hatchers and the Pritchetts, for all those who'd had to destroy their herds in order to hang on to the farms and ranches that were supported by that livestock. She wept over the cruel and bizarre irony of that.

She wept for poor Doralee Gerald, who would probably grow old without her unhappy situation ever changing, who would always be an object of either pity or ridicule. She even shed compassionate tears for the lawyer, Mr. Whitehead, whom she barely knew but who seemed like a decent man trapped in a moral dilemma and hopelessly sad circumstances.

Eventually her tears subsided, and she brought the sobs under control. This morning she had prided herself on being able to contain her tears. But lately, that ability had deserted her. Bouts of weeping were becoming more frequent and exponentially turbulent. She'd cried that night in Solly's room following his fit over the spools that had interrupted the gentlemen's chess game. She'd been reduced to tears last night when Mr. Rainwater gave her the book. Tonight's sobbing had been the most extreme emotional outburst so far. She must reverse this trend. Starting now.

She went inside and locked the screened door, then went through the house checking the other doors and turning out lights. In her room, she undressed down to her slip and pulled on her summer-weight wrapper. Ashamed of her red, swollen eyes, she bathed them with cold water until they looked more normal, then cleaned her teeth and finally pulled the pins from her hair and uncoiled the heavy bun.

She was turning down her bed when the knock on her door came, so softly that, at first, she thought she had imagined it. But it came again, just as softly, but undeniably.

Making certain that her wrapper was securely belted, she went to the door and opened it a crack. "Mr. Rainwater." Instantly concerned, she opened the door wider and looked him up and down, wondering if the difficulty in his side had been more than a stitch, if he was more than just winded. "Are you ill?"

"I heard you crying."

"Oh."

"My room is just above the porch."

"Oh. Yes."

"My windows were open."

"I didn't think. I'm sorry if I disturbed you."

"You didn't. Not in the way you mean." He paused a beat, then asked her why she'd been crying.

"It was silly."

He said nothing, just stood there looking down into her face, patiently, or stubbornly, waiting for her to explain.

She made a helpless gesture. "Several reasons."

"Like what?"

"There just seems to be . . ."

"What?"

"So much cruelty, and pain, and sadness in life. And I was just wondering why that is." Of course the ultimate unfairness was his circumstance. The reminder of that brought fresh tears to her eyes, which she impatiently wiped away with the back of her hand. "Thank you for your concern, but I'm fine."

"Are you?"

She looked into his eyes, but her nod of affirmation must not have been convincing, because he didn't move. Nor did she. They continued to stare at each other until she began to feel the same tightness in her chest that she'd felt last night when she'd held the gift of his book in her hands, until her veins throbbed with blood suddenly gone feverish, until her eyes stung with fresh tears, and she had to clamp her teeth over her lower lip to keep it from trembling.

He took a step nearer. She saw her name, *Ella,* form on his lips, but she couldn't hear it for her pulse drumming in her ears.

Slowly, he raised his hands and placed one on each side of her face, curving them to fit her cheeks. He lowered his head. Feeling his breath warm on her face, she made a weak mewling sound. He touched his lips to the corner of her mouth.

Her breath caught.

Then he kissed the other corner of her lips. She closed her eyes, squeezing out tears that felt very wet, very hot on her cheeks.

"Don't cry," he whispered.

The brush of his lips across hers sparked a longing deep within. It didn't unfurl gradually, or come to life drowsily after its long repose. It erupted. So that when he kissed her mouth fully, she began making such hungry sounds, he backed her into the room and gently closed the door with his foot.

With the door at his back for support, he pulled her to him, and for the longest time, they clung to each other. She reveled in the feel of his arms around her, his breath quick against her neck. She leaned into him, feeling his hard bones and the solidness of his form in thrilling contrast to the softness of hers.

She pressed her face into the vee of his open collar and touched his throat with her lips. His skin was warm. She breathed deeply of his smell, so familiar to her now, but so very forbidden until this moment, when she didn't deny herself indulging in it, drinking it in, taking it into herself, committing it to memory for life.

He eased her away and combed his hands through her hair, watching as the undisciplined strands celebrated their freedom by coiling themselves around his fingers. He seemed fascinated by the abundance of her hair, its texture and length, and she got the sense that he would enjoy playing with it for hours.

Then his eyes settled on hers. His remarkable eyes. Blue and pure, the most beautiful eyes she had ever seen, or would ever see again in her lifetime. She would vow to that.

"I love you, Ella."

She closed her eyes for a brief few seconds, and when she opened them again, she whispered shakily, "I know."

"I would never do anything to damage you."

"No, you wouldn't."

"So if you tell me to leave, I will."

She laid her cheek against his chest. "If you left me now, I wouldn't survive my regret."

He sighed her name as he tilted her face up and slanted his lips across hers.

Ella thought she might die of the pleasure that coursed through her. But then he lowered his hands from her face and untied the belt of her wrapper. When his hands were inside it, bracketing her rib cage, and she could feel the pressure of each of his long fingers, she realized that his kiss was only a prelude to the pleasure he could give her. And when he moved his hands up and down over the slippery fabric of her slip and they brushed the undersides of her breasts, she became certain of it.

She didn't have a mirror, and it would have been too dark in the bedroom to see her reflection anyway, but she knew that, as she gazed into his face, her eyes must have been glassy with wonder. "I had no idea."

He was equally intent on his study of her face. "What?"

"That I could feel, that *anyone* could feel, something that extraordinary, and live through it. How is it possible?"

"It was one of the Creator's finest hours."

She smiled and nuzzled his shoulder, then laid her head on

it. "It was nothing like that with my husband. So unlike it I can't even compare the two experiences. I didn't love him. Perhaps that's why."

"If you didn't love him, why did you marry him?"

"I'd already rejected Conrad. I suppose I was afraid that, if I continued turning down suitors, I soon wouldn't have any. I didn't want to wind up the old-maid landlady of a boarding-house." Pensively, she added, "Of course that's what happened. Essentially."

"You have Solly."

"Yes."

Mr. Rainwater took a strand of her hair and rubbed it between his fingers. "Your husband must not have loved you, either, Ella. If he had, he wouldn't have left you."

"He loved me, I think. In his way. The best way he knew how. But he just couldn't handle what was happening to Solly. Maybe he was frustrated because he was powerless to fix it. Maybe he considered Solly a poor reflection on him. Or perhaps he looked into the future and saw what having a child like Solly would mean to our lives, and he simply had to escape. But I don't suppose I'll ever know for certain what drove him to leave."

"You don't know if he's dead or alive?"

She shook her head, then lifted it from his shoulder and, looking down on him, smiled wanly. "It's likely that I'm an adulteress. Willfully and gladly I've committed that sin tonight." Her eyes began to fill. "Is loving you God's way of punishing me?"

He touched her lips with his fingertips, then drew her to him, saying, "No, Ella, no. It's His blessing."

⁂

It was inevitable—morning came.

As the eastern sky began to turn gray, Ella woke up. She lay perfectly still, reveling in the feel of him against her, in the gentle sound of his breathing, in the knowledge that, if she lived to be a century old, she would never forget the sweetness of this dawn.

Begrudgingly, she woke him. He groaned a protest but knew he had to leave her room before they were discovered. They got the giggles as he searched in the dark for his clothes, and then he buttoned his shirt wrong, and she had to unbutton it and do it for him.

"Hurry," she said, stifling her laughter as she hustled him toward the door and passed him his shoes. "You don't want the Dunne sisters to catch you sneaking out of my bedroom."

"How do you know I haven't been sneaking out of theirs since I moved in?"

That set her off again, and she had to cover her mouth to trap the giggles inside. He removed her hand and tried to kiss her, but she dodged it. "Go! I want to take a bath before I start the day."

"You feel unclean?"

"No, I feel sore." Even in the dim light, she saw his grin. Slapping his arm softly, she said, "Don't look so pleased with yourself." He kissed her again before she could protest, and when the playfulness of it began quickly to evolve into a kiss of a different sort, she pushed him away. "If you want biscuits for breakfast—"

"I'm going."

He was the first to come downstairs. He had washed, shaved, and changed clothes. Her eyes gobbled him up, and she continued to be greedy for the sight of him, resenting each time she had to return to the kitchen while serving breakfast.

She missed Margaret's helping hands, but, despite the reason for her absence, Ella was glad she wasn't there this morning. Surely Margaret would have sensed the change in her, in the house, in everything.

The atmosphere crackled with invisible currents each time she and Mr. Rainwater made eye contact. Whenever she was near him, she craved to touch him, and only the strongest act of will kept her from doing so. She knew he was feeling similarly; he looked at her with patent yearning, his eyes following every motion.

The spinster sisters seemed oblivious to the dramatic differences between yesterday and today, which Ella found incredible. To her it was obvious that nothing smelled or tasted or sounded or looked or felt or *was* the same as it had been only hours ago.

She swore she could feel her blood coursing through her veins as though dams that had been holding it back all her life had been opened, unlocked by Mr. Rainwater's touch. All five senses were heightened. Her nerve endings were sensitized. Her body tingled and ached deliciously, in a way it never had before.

Were these overpowering physical sensations what the preachers called lust? If so, she now realized why they were warned against from pulpits around the world. They were more powerful than the sweetest narcotic, more intoxicating than the strongest liquor. She now understood how easily and happily one would relinquish control to them until they governed one's whole being.

Little had she known, or ever even imagined, that what

men and women did together could be so breathtakingly sweet, so beautiful to body, mind, and soul.

She finished her chores as quickly as possible so she could spend time with him and Solly. After lunch, he invented an errand for himself and invited her and Solly to go along. It was a contrivance to get the three of them out of the house and alone, leaving the Dunnes with a plausible explanation for their absence.

They drove into the countryside and found a shady, pleasant spot in a grove of pecan trees that grew alongside a creek. There they spread a quilt. For a time, Mr. Rainwater engaged Solly in card games that he made up as he went along, and they marveled at the progress he'd made.

"He's grasping concepts, Ella," he said excitedly when Solly responded successfully to a challenge. "I'm sure of it."

"So am I."

She was equally sure that Solly wouldn't have come this far if not for Mr. Rainwater, and that made her feel both ashamed for her failure and grateful for his kind interference. She was no longer jealous of it, only immensely thankful.

They could not, however, coax Solly to wade into the creek with them. He got visibly upset when they tried to remove his shoes, so they returned to the quilt and gave him the deck of cards. He played with them while Mr. Rainwater laid his head in Ella's lap and read aloud to her from the Hemingway novel.

At one point, he stopped, tilted his head back, and, seeing the tears in her eyes, said, "This isn't even the sad part."

"I'm not crying over the story, or because I'm sad." She looked at Solly as he stared up into the branches of the tree, seemingly fixated on the patterns the leaves formed against the sky. Those same patterns were reflected in Mr. Rainwater's eyes when she returned her gaze to him. "I don't remember a single moment of my life when I've been this happy or content. And it's because of you."

He sat up and placed his arms around her. They kissed, chastely. But for the remainder of the time, they sat with their arms wrapped around each other, basking in the hazy heat of the afternoon and in the love they'd found when they least expected it.

Ella had to rush to get dinner on the table by six-thirty and guiltily used Margaret's absence as an excuse for it being a cold supper of sliced ham and various salads. The Dunnes didn't seem to mind, probably because Mr. Rainwater paid them extra attention and drew them into a conversation about the differences between schoolchildren today and the students they had taught decades earlier. Was there indeed evidence of moral decay among America's youth? The discussion that followed distracted them from not having a hot meal.

As Ella was finishing up the dishes, Jimmy came to the back door with a message. "Brother Calvin's funeral is tomorrow at five o'clock."

"Why so late in the day?"

"So they can have dinner on the grounds after."

It was a term used for picnics usually held after Sunday services when people tended to the graves of loved ones in the adjacent cemetery. Food was brought and shared in the churchyard.

"The funeral is at the church?"

"Seemed fittin'."

Ella supposed it did, although she didn't know how anyone could enter that sanctuary without thinking of the young minister's body hanging from the beam. Maybe the funeral was an attempt to purify it, rid it of that stigma. "How is your mother?"

"She's heartbroke."

"All of us are."

"Meanin' no disrespect, Miss Ella. But not all."

Later, she recounted the conversation to Mr. Rainwater. "I'm worried about Jimmy and other young men. I hope they won't try and get revenge."

"I hope they won't, either, because that would only create more trouble, probably bloodshed. But since they've been denied justice, one could hardly blame them if they wanted vengeance."

Ella's concerns were justified later that evening.

She and Mr. Rainwater were sitting apart in the parlor, waiting in an agony of anticipation for the Dunne sisters to retire, when he set aside the magazine he was reading and went to the front window. "Something's burning."

Ella put down her mending and joined him at the window. The flames could be seen against the night sky. "Something near the highway."

Just then the telephone rang. As Ella walked toward the back of the staircase to answer it, Miss Pearl appeared in the arched opening of the informal parlor. "Mrs. Barron, we smell smoke."

"Something in town is on fire."

"Oh, dear," whimpered Miss Violet, who joined her sister, holding her hand of cards in her age-spotted grip.

Ella answered the phone. It was Ollie Thompson, and she held her breath, fearing that he would ask to speak to Mr. Rainwater and summon him to the scene of another crisis. But he was only calling to pass along information. She thanked him and hung up. After replacing the telephone, she turned to find her three boarders in the hallway, waiting to hear the news.

"That was Ollie. He knew we had probably smelled the smoke. He called to tell us that the fire is at Packy Simpson's auto garage."

"Oh, what a shame," Miss Pearl said. "He's such a nice nigra. Always tips his hat to us, doesn't he, Sister?"

Ignoring them, Ella looked at Mr. Rainwater, who asked, "How did it start?"

"The sheriff accused him of leaving a cigarette burning in an ashtray when he closed up shop. Mr. Simpson dips snuff. He doesn't smoke." She let that sink in, then said, "His business is a total loss, but he's glad the fire didn't spread to his house. The two buildings are separated by only twenty yards."

The sisters drifted back into the informal parlor to finish their gin game. Ella motioned Mr. Rainwater back into the front room. Solly was where she'd left him, sitting on the rug stacking spools. "Mr. Simpson is a deacon at Brother Calvin's church," she said in a voice that the spinsters couldn't overhear. "He's a pallbearer for the funeral tomorrow."

Mr. Rainwater looked at her for several moments, then asked, "Where was Ollie calling from?"

"The drugstore. People had congregated there to watch the fire. He knew we'd want to know."

He turned and headed toward the front door. Ella rushed after him. "You're going?"

"I want to talk to whoever's still at the drugstore, see what I can learn. It can't be a coincidence that a Negro's business burns down the night after another was lynched."

She agreed, of course, but her heart constricted with anxiety. "Please don't go."

"I won't be long." He put on his hat.

"You're favoring your side."

"What?"

"All afternoon, I've noticed, but I didn't want to make you angry by asking about it. It's hurting you, isn't it?"

"I'm fine."

"Let me call Dr. Kincaid."

He smiled at her frantic attempt to keep him there. "I won't be long."

As he stepped through the door, she grabbed his arm. "Promise me you'll be careful."

"I promise." He glanced behind her to see that the coast was clear, then whispered, "I'll see you later."

EIGHTEEN

It was later—much later—when she heard his car. By that time she had put Solly down for the night, finished her mending and preparations for tomorrow's meals, and whipped herself into a full-blown panic, which he dispelled the instant she unlocked the screened door to let him in.

"I'm all right. When the drugstore closed, some of us hung around, making ourselves visible in the hope there wouldn't be any more incidents tonight. There weren't."

"Thank heaven for that."

"Yes, but the general consensus is that the fire was set as a warning to anyone in the Negro community who might be plotting revenge for Brother Calvin. As you might guess, Mr. Simpson had been rather outspoken about the lynching. There was a prayer meeting held at noon today. He prayed that God's wrath would rain down on those guilty of his pastor's murder. Which, by the way, Sheriff Anderson ruled a suicide."

"That's ludicrous."

"Everyone knows better. That's why tension is so high."

While Ella was worried about the volatile situation, she was selfishly relieved to have Mr. Rainwater back safe and sound. She wanted to throw her arms around him and tell him so, but a wavering voice came from the top of the stairs.

"Is everything all right in town, Mrs. Barron?"

She turned to see not one, but both, of the Dunne sisters peering at them over the banister. "Yes. Fine," she said, struggling to keep the disappointment out of her voice. She'd been hoping that Mr. Rainwater could come directly to her room upon his return. Now, that was impossible. She was being cheated of time with him, and she wanted to rant over it. Instead, she said calmly, "Mr. Rainwater has just come back."

He headed for the staircase. "Ladies, I'm pleased to report that the fire is out and that it was contained to one structure. It's a sad loss for Mr. Simpson, but at least there were no casualties."

The sisters murmured their agreement.

He was halfway up the staircase before he glanced down at Ella. "I apologize for making you wait up to let me in, Mrs. Barron."

"I would have been up anyway, Mr. Rainwater. Good night."

It was the longest hour of Ella's life, because each minute that passed was one that she didn't have with him. She despaired that, once he reached his room, he'd been overcome with fatigue and fallen asleep. The thought of having to forfeit a night with him almost brought her to tears.

She didn't recognize this hysteria in herself. Twenty-four hours ago, she had been a circumspect lady, conscientious of each stray curl that escaped her bun, worried over the impropriety of accepting his gift of a book, uneasy with his using her given name, fretful over being seen riding with him in his car. Now she was afraid that he wouldn't share her bed again.

When he knocked, she practically flew across the room. She opened the door; he slipped in. "Did they hear you?"

"I don't think so."

She was seized by a sudden shyness, barely breathing, trying to make out his shape in the darkness. But then he reached for her and pulled her to him. When their lips met, her timidity dissolved.

Their desire for each other was such that they didn't even undress, which made the fevered coupling seem even more illicit than it had last night, when they'd slowly, almost reverently, helped each other remove their clothing before lying down together. Somehow, disrobing had seemed more decorous than now, when their groping and grappling through their clothes produced moans of pleasure mixed with frustration.

Only afterward did they undress. But their nakedness stirred their passions again, and their hands couldn't remain still. When kisses left them breathless, his mouth moved to her breasts. She enfolded his head in her arms and held him fast, wishing that her breasts had milk so that she could nurture him, sustain him, heal him.

The grief overcame her suddenly and cruelly. She began to sob. "Don't leave me."

He raised his head and touched her cheeks, feeling tears.

Her hands clutched at him. "You can't. You can't leave me."

"Ssh, Ella."

"Oh, dear God, please." She hugged him tightly, a bit mad in her desperation to hold on to him absolutely and forever. "I can't bear it if you leave me. Say you won't. Swear you won't."

"Ssh. Ssh." He held her against him, rocking her in his arms like a child, rubbing his lips against her hair. "Don't ask me for the one thing I can't give you, Ella. If I could, I would. But the one thing I can't give you is time."

He continued to hold her until she quieted. When he eventually pulled back so he could look at her, he brushed strands of hair off her face and ran his thumbs across her cheeks. "This is the first time, as well as the last time, I've loved. And it's perfect, Ella. Perfect."

Her heart was full to bursting, so full she couldn't speak, but he understood what she felt without her having to say a word.

He understood everything.

In the morning, she was ashamed of that outburst. She had asked the impossible of him, and knew that it broke his heart as much as it did hers that he couldn't grant her fervent wish. But dwelling on her emotional breakdown, and chastising herself for it, would have been an even greater waste of their time together. So she pushed it from her mind and thought instead of the miracle of making love with him and to him. Loving him was the dearest of gifts.

Following breakfast, he offered to assist her with the cleanup, and she accepted. Not because she needed the help in Margaret's absence but so they could share a room. He kept an eye on Solly while she did general housekeeping. A few days ago, it would have been vastly important to her that a tabletop was polished just so, or that each corner was thoroughly swept.

But her priorities had changed. She did only what was necessary to keep the house tidy and nothing more, not wanting to spend her time scrubbing when she could be looking at Mr.

Rainwater instead. That was really all she wanted to do: look at him and record for memory his smile, the disobedient lock of hair, the various inflections of his voice, each eyelash, and every line in the palms of his hands.

After lunch, she fried two chickens, made potato salad, and baked a cake to contribute to the meal following Brother Calvin's funeral service. Mr. Rainwater stayed in the kitchen with her while she worked, helping with the chopping and slicing. Solly played at the table.

Ella pretended . . . Well, she pretended lots of things.

When the picnic food was ready, Mr. Rainwater went to his room to change clothes. Ella dressed herself and Solly in their Sunday best.

"Well, don't you look nice, Solly," Miss Pearl exclaimed when Ella walked hand in hand with him into the parlor where the sisters were listening to a concert on the radio.

Again, Ella marveled that they detected nothing out of the ordinary. How could that be, when everything was so radically different? The changes that loving Mr. Rainwater had wrought were so vital, she couldn't believe they were undetectable. Even when they were apart, she felt his body against hers, as though it had left an indelible imprint on her. She wondered how it could possibly be invisible.

"The table is set, and a platter of fried chicken is on the kitchen table," she told the two sisters. "Potato salad, cucumber salad, and tea are in the icebox. If I've forgotten something, please help yourselves. Leave your dishes. I'll clean up when we get back."

"I still question if it's . . . appropriate for you to attend this funeral, Mrs. Barron." Miss Violet's expression was one of a reproving schoolteacher. Her lips were pursed so tightly, Ella wondered how she was able to enunciate.

"Sister's right, Mrs. Barron. It might not be safe," Miss Pearl added, for some reason whispering.

"We'll be perfectly safe."

Miss Violet released a long sigh. "Well, if you're determined to go . . ."

"I am."

"Then I'm glad Mr. Rainwater will be by your side."

"I'm glad of that, too," Ella said.

He appeared then, carrying the picnic hamper and a cake box. Ella took the box from him. "You ladies enjoy your evening," he said, tipping his hat. Then he escorted Ella and Solly out the front door and to his car.

They were early, but the church was already packed when they arrived. Cars and mule-drawn wagons were lined up along the street for blocks in both directions. Every pew in the sanctuary was filled. Standing room also proved inadequate, so there was a spillover crowd standing in the churchyard, looking in through the windows.

Many of the people Ella recognized from shantytown had chosen to remain outside. Some whites, too, apparently shared the Dunne sisters' reservations about attending. They were there, but they stayed clumped together and segregated for the most part. Her heart warmed to see Lola and Ollie Thompson and Mr. and Mrs. Pritchett among those who went inside.

Because of the circumstances of the preacher's death, Ella had thought there would be law enforcement officers nearby to guard against a disturbance rising from any quarter, but she saw no one in uniform.

Mr. Rainwater found the absence of lawmen unusual, too, and remarked on it. "Since the sheriff is in cahoots with the criminals, I had hoped he would keep his distance. But I'm surprised that he did. I would have thought he and his deputies would be camped nearby, if for no other reason than to intimidate. Or even to gloat."

Jimmy appeared in the open doorway of the sanctuary and waved them inside, where Margaret had saved them seats. Ella feared that Solly might panic when he was jammed in between her and Mr. Rainwater, but when he began flapping his hands at his ears and showing the initial signs of a fit, Mr. Rainwater took several nickels from his pants pocket and scattered them upon the worn cover of a hymnal. Solly focused on them immediately and began rearranging the coins to his liking.

Ella smiled across the top of her son's head at Mr. Rainwater. He smiled back.

Ella had attended the funeral service for Margaret's husband, so she wasn't surprised by the vocal outpourings of grief. Brother Calvin's young widow was inconsolable. The choir sang long and loud. It seemed that everyone who had ever known the preacher had been invited to give a eulogy, and after the scheduled speakers had had their time at the pulpit, anyone who felt led to speak was invited to do so, and many did. The visiting preacher's homily escalated into a lengthy sermon.

Miraculously, Solly remained quiet and docile, occupied with the coins throughout the service. Ella's underclothing grew damp with perspiration. She used the hand fan that she'd been given when she came in, but it was insufficient. The heat inside the church became more intense as the service progressed.

However, her own discomfort was nothing compared to Mr. Rainwater's. At first, she'd become aware of his fidgeting.

Then she noticed him frequently reaching inside his suit coat to rub his side. His face grew pale and bathed with sweat, which he dabbed at with a handkerchief, sometimes pressing it hard against his lips.

He caught her watching him and smiled reassuringly. "Just a twinge," he mouthed.

But she knew it was more than that. As much as she'd admired Brother Calvin, she wished for a swift conclusion to the service so she could take Mr. Rainwater home. She would insist he give himself a shot to relieve the evident pain he was suffering. Perhaps they should stop at Dr. Kincaid's office before they went home.

As soon as the last amen was said, Ella maneuvered Solly into the aisle, paying no heed to his squealing protests when she scooped up his nickels. "I'll leave the food we brought," she said to Mr. Rainwater when they were stopped by the logjam of mourners at the door. "But let's not stay. Let's go home."

"Why? Solly feels claustrophobic because of the crowd. He'll calm down once we're outside."

"It's not Solly I'm worried about. I know you're in pain."

"I'm fine." Seeing her consternation, he surreptitiously reached for her hand and squeezed it. "I'm all right, and it would hurt Margaret's feelings if we didn't stay."

So they stayed. There was no grave-site service because Brother Calvin's coffin was being transported to Houston for burial. Tables were set up beneath the trees shading the church-yard. While Mr. Rainwater minded Solly, Ella added their food to what others had brought.

The people of shantytown began to leave, but Mr. Simpson, the deacon whose building had been destroyed the night before, stood on a tree stump and announced that everyone was invited to stay and partake of the meal even if they hadn't contributed. The people who had come empty-handed were hesitant to accept the charitable invitation, but ultimately their embarrassment wasn't as strong as their hunger pangs, and they shuffled to get in line.

"Not as good as yours," Mr. Rainwater said as he bit into a fried chicken drumstick. "But word must have got around. The platter you brought was empty."

They'd gone through the line to get their food, then Ella had spread a quilt on a grassy spot at the edge of the churchyard. He appeared to be feeling somewhat better. He wasn't sweating as profusely, but there was still a sheen of perspiration on his face. His complexion looked waxy, and his lips were rimmed with white. He looked as he had the day she'd discovered him lying in his bed suffering excruciating pain.

"You're not hungry?" he asked, nodding down at her plate. She'd barely nibbled at the food.

"It's the heat, I think." But it wasn't the temperature. It was him. She was worried sick about him.

He saw through her fib. "Don't fret over me, Ella."

"I can't help it."

"I love you for your concern, but I don't want to cause you one moment of heartache. Ever."

Peering deeply into his eyes, she said hoarsely, "You will."

He returned the drumstick to his plate. Staring into near space, he said, "Then I should never have come to you."

She shook her head furiously. "No. Oh no. It would have been like not reading the book because of the sad ending. I had a choice." Not caring who saw, she reached out and stroked his cheek until his eyes met hers again. "I wouldn't have missed loving you. Not for anything in the world."

They gazed at each other, communicating without words, apart from their environment, unmindful of anything going on around them. The spell was broken when, simultaneously, they became aware of Solly's restlessness. "He needs the bathroom." She stood up and took her son's hand.

"Where's the nearest one?"

"It's an outhouse, I'm afraid. Behind the church. I'll be right back."

"I'll clean up here and meet you at the car."

It was deep twilight by now. Stars were out. The moon was a china plate rising above the rooftops. The crowd had thinned considerably. Even those who had stayed to take down the tables and collect dishes and trash had departed. She had been so wrapped up with Mr. Rainwater, she hadn't noticed.

Jimmy and Margaret drove past in his ancient jalopy. Margaret waved, calling out, "I'll see you in the morning, bright and early."

Hurrying Solly along, Ella led him by the hand down the side of the church toward the rear of the building. The two outhouses were a distance from the sanctuary. One was marked for men, the other for women. Ella knew that one would be as bad as the other, and she dreaded taking Solly into either.

It was dark behind the church, where the area was enclosed by tall shrubbery. She considered letting him go in the bushes but knew that he would balk because of his innate fastidiousness. Besides that, she didn't want to risk him being seen making water in the outdoors. If a normal boy did, people would smile and say boys would be boys. If Solly were caught doing it, there was no telling what the repercussions would be. It could be said that, because he wasn't right in the head, he was a deviant.

The stench assailed her when she opened the flimsy door to the women's outhouse. Holding her breath, she guided Solly inside. The cubicle was dark, which was probably a blessing, but it was a disadvantage to her getting his shorts unbuttoned. That accomplished, she stood him in front of the hole. He was barely tall enough for the stream to clear the bench, but he did his business without mishap.

Hastily she buttoned up his shorts. "Good job, Solly. Good job." She must remember to scrub both their hands with soap and hot water as soon as they got home. If she could convince Mr. Rainwater to stop at Dr. Kincaid's house on the way, they could wash there.

Determined to persuade Mr. Rainwater to see the doctor tonight, she pushed Solly through the outhouse door and quickly closed it behind her.

"Hey, Ella."

Startled, she spun around. Conrad Ellis was there, his shoulder casually propped against the exterior wall of the building. The deputy's badge was pinned to a uniform shirt, and he was wearing a leather holster with a pistol in it. His birthmark looked as dark as ink in the faint light. A cigarette dangled from his lips, which formed an insolent smile.

He tilted his head toward the small enclosure. "Niggers sure know how to stink up a place, don't they?"

"What are you doing here?"

"Official duty," he said, tapping the grip of the pistol with his index finger like a gunfighter about to draw. "Keeping the niggers from running amok."

Ella's heart was beating hard and fast, but she realized the worst thing she could do was to show him her fear. She took

Solly firmly by the hand and started walking quickly away.

But Conrad wasn't having it. He stepped in front of her, blocking her path. "What's with you these days? You think your shit *don't* stink? You're too good to say a polite hello to old friends?"

"If I say a polite hello will you get out of my way?"

He took the cigarette from his mouth and threw it in the grass, grinding it out with the toe of his shoe even as he took a step closer to her. "Depends."

"On what?"

He leered. "On how polite you're willing to get."

Instantly she understood his intention. She opened her mouth to scream, but he lunged and slammed her into the wall of the outhouse, clamping one of his hands over her mouth.

Something landed hard on the ground beside her, and she realized that, in his forward motion, Conrad had also knocked Solly aside. The way Conrad had her pinned against the outhouse wall made it impossible for her to move her arms, but she extended her fingers as far as she could, groping hopelessly to touch her son even as she struggled to free her mouth from Conrad's hand. Overpowering him was impossible, but if she could scream, someone would hear her.

"You should be nicer to me, Ella, you really should." All insouciance gone now, he was panting like an animal. "Like you're nice to that boarder you've got. How come you're giving him what you never gave me, huh?" His damp breath smelled of whiskey, but she was powerless to turn her face away.

A sound of outrage issued from her throat when he squeezed her breast with his free hand, but that only made him maul her more roughly. "How come you like that pale pantywaist instead of me? If you wanted a man, why didn't you call on me?"

234   SANDRA BROWN

He managed to work his hand between their bodies and push it between her legs. She tried to evade his crude thrusting motions, but she couldn't back up, and he was pressed against her so solidly, she couldn't move from side to side. The unforgiving buckle of his holster was gouging her belly.

And Solly, was he hurt? When he was shoved to the ground, had he been knocked unconscious? Looking out the corner of her eye, she tried to see him, but her entire field of vision was filled with Conrad's face, congested with rage, bloated from liquor, his small eyes smoldering with resentment and cruelty.

She heard, coming from somewhere not too distant, the sound of revving engines, a sharp whistle, and then someone calling Conrad's name. Either he didn't hear it or he ignored it. Grunting with the effort, he pushed her feet apart with his, making it impossible for her to close her legs. To her horror, she realized that he was fumbling with his fly and muttering curses of frustration when he couldn't get it open.

Her mind was screaming, *This cannot be happening to me.* But it was, it *would*, if she didn't stop it.

Suddenly, she ceased struggling and went limp. Confused, Conrad staggered back. It was only a few inches, and he relaxed his hold on her only marginally, but Ella used that split second of his befuddlement to cram her knee into his crotch.

He opened his mouth to scream, but only a thin gasp of agony came out. He clutched his groin with both hands and dropped to his knees, then toppled facefirst onto the ground. Ella covered her face with her hands, partially to block out the sight and sound of him as he writhed in pain at her feet, partially to regain her breath, slow down her pounding heart, and pull herself together.

She heard the rumble of racing motors coming nearer, the squeal of tires, men laughing and whooping drunkenly. Conrad's crowd. Closing in. She had to move, get away from him before his friends arrived. But she couldn't move just yet. She needed a few more seconds to collect her wits.

"Ella?"

Her name. Shouted in Mr. Rainwater's voice. His dear, dear voice. It was a blessed sound reaching her despite Conrad's choked sobs.

"Ella?"

Conrad's groans intensified.

And then there was another sound. An abrupt cracking sound that was inexplicably wet-sounding, like the splat of a ripe melon being busted open.

Conrad's moaning abruptly ceased.

Ella lowered her hands from her face.

Conrad still lay on the ground at her feet. But he was no longer moving. The back of his head had been split right down the center of his skull. It was too dark now to distinguish color, but the lumpy matter inside the crevasse glistened, and the liquid spilling out of it and pooling on the ground appeared as black as motor oil reflecting the moonlight.

Over him stood Solly, a large, bloodstained stone in his hands.

Ella clapped her hand over her mouth, although she continued to make strange cooing sounds of profound horror. She sank to her knees, looking in turn at Conrad's gaping skull and her son's placid, angelic face.

"Ella!"

She saw Mr. Rainwater's shoes skid to a stop beside Conrad's still form. His breath left his body in an audible gush. He knelt beside Solly, and Ella watched as he removed from her son's small hands the stone with which Conrad Ellis had been brained. Only then did she raise her eyes to meet Mr. Rainwater's and saw in them the disbelief and alarm that matched hers.

"Good job, Solly."

In unison, they turned and stared aghast at the boy, who'd spoken the words. He was staring down at the damage he'd wreaked, having no comprehension of what it signified except an end to suffering, and speaking the words of commendation that recently had so often been repeated to him. They had penetrated his mind, had been recorded, and now he called them forth. "Good job, Solly. Good job, Solly. Good job, Solly."

"Oh *God!*" Ella crawled over to him and clasped him against her, pressing his face against her breasts, muffling his incriminating litany. Having lived for the day she would hear him speak, now she wanted to shush his sweet voice, silence that chant that would condemn him. "Ssh, Solly. Ssh. No, baby, no."

On the street in front of the church, they heard shouts and laughter, the slamming of car doors, breaking glass, running footsteps. Lantern light flickered through the trees.

Someone called in a singsong voice, "Con-rad? Where are you?"

"Come out, come out, wherever you are."

"Let's go nigger knockin'!"

Solly was now screeching and trying to escape Ella's grasp. His hands were flapping at his ears like the wings of an injured bird. Above his head, she frantically looked at Mr. Rainwater. Their gazes locked and held for no longer than a few seconds.

And then he did the oddest thing.

He dipped his hands in the blood that had collected under Conrad's head.

Ella gaped at him with bafflement as he slowly came to his feet, the stone in his hands, and turned toward the onrushing group of men who were now rounding the corner of the church, led by the sheriff himself.

Still several yards away, one of the men drew up short. "What the hell? Conrad?"

One by one, the others saw what had brought their friend to a standstill. They stared at Ella, Solly, and Mr. Rainwater, trying to register what their minds refused to accept.

Then the pack surged forward as one, yelling and cursing. Two of them tackled Mr. Rainwater, following him down when he fell and pummeling him with their fists.

"Stop! No!" Ella screamed. "Leave him alone."

But nobody was listening to her. They were like rabid dogs, salivating, waiting their turn at Mr. Rainwater.

"Hold off, hold off!" Sheriff Anderson elbowed his way through them, pushing bodies aside, until he hauled the last man off Mr. Rainwater. Gripping him beneath his arms, the sheriff pulled him to his feet. But he couldn't stand on his own, so two of the men held him upright while the sheriff jerked his bloody hands behind his back and cuffed them. His head was bowed low over his chest. A ribbon of blood hung from his lower lip. He swayed on his feet.

Ella, finally grasping what was happening, made a low keening sound, then croaked, "No."

The sheriff turned to her. "One of these men will see you and your boy home, Mrs. Barron. They'll stay with you till I get this character locked up. Then I'll come around to question you."

"No! Mr. Rainwater didn't do anything."

"Ella."

"It wasn't—"

"Ella."

Wildly her eyes swung to him who spoke her name as no one else ever had. His head was raised now. He was looking directly at her. Quietly he said, "Do as the sheriff says. This is the way it's to be."

Realization of what he meant to do came to her slowly as she stood there breathing hard, sobbing dryly. Furiously, she shook her head. "No!"

As distraught as she was, he was perfectly composed. "It's all right."

She looked down at Solly, who, since she had released him, had calmed down and was no longer screeching but was still flapping his hands at the sides of his head and chanting in a whisper, "Good job, Solly."

Then she looked back at the man who'd touched her son, reached him, when no one else had, even she.

She looked at the man who had touched her.

His image began to waver as her eyes filled. Again she shook her head, saying feebly, "No, no."

His eyes had never looked more serene. Certainly never more loving. Slowly he nodded. His lips moved, and she read the word on them. *Yes*.

EPILOGUE

"He died before they could execute him."

The couple hadn't moved for the past hour. The afternoon was leaning toward dusk, but the passage of time had gone unnoticed. The woman was sniffing. Her husband passed her his handkerchief. She thanked him and daintily blotted her nose.

"That's his pocket watch?" she asked. "Mr. Rainwater's."

The antiques dealer nodded. "He asked Dr. Kincaid to have it engraved with the date on which the doctor brought him to my mother's house and introduced them." He fingered the characters etched into the gold. "After the sheriff took him away that night, they never saw each other again."

"Surely she attended his trial," the woman said.

"There wasn't a trial. He confessed. He refused to see her in prison. He didn't want to leave her with that memory of him. Dr. Kincaid carried messages back and forth between them."

"How long did he live?" the man asked.

"Five weeks. He didn't have to suffer for long."

The lady reached for her husband's hand and clasped it tightly. "Your mother probably suffered more than he did."

"She desperately wanted to see him, but later she came to understand that, as usual, he knew what was best. She told me she didn't think she could have survived watching him die."

"How did she ever recover?"

"After he died, she was shocked to learn that he'd bequeathed everything to her. Not all those afternoon absences were spent with Ollie Thompson and Brother Calvin. Some were spent getting his affairs in order." The old man smiled. "Mother was well ahead of her time and put the legacy to good use. As soon as it was practical, she closed the boardinghouse and moved to North Texas, where she started replanting cotton on Mr. Rainwater's land. Harvested it, ginned it, sold it. Brokered for other planters, too, just like he had.

"A few years later, she used the profits to build a textile plant. She became quite wealthy, and well respected. She received, oh, I can't even remember all the citations and awards. Outstanding businesswoman, citizen of the year, commendations like that."

"Remarkable," the woman said with awe.

"She was, actually." Again the old man fingered the watch wistfully. "She told me once it had taken a dying man to teach her how to live. Before Mr. Rainwater, she'd been resigned to a life of virtual imprisonment. He freed her. In every way."

"He was remarkable in his own right," the man observed. "He died a condemned man when he was blameless. I realize he would have died soon anyway. Still, he made a huge sacrifice for you."

The old man divided a puzzled look between them, then

realized it was they who were confused. "He made the sacrifice for *Solly*."

"But . . . aren't you . . . ?"

He shook his head.

The woman glanced down at the business card he'd given her. "I assumed . . . The name of your shop—"

"Is in honor of my brother. My name is David. David Rainwater Barron."

They looked at him with dismay. "You're his son?" the woman whispered.

"I am."

She began crying again, this time with joy. Her husband placed his arm around her. He asked, "What happened to Solly?"

"After moving to North Texas, Mother checked into a school in Dallas. It had a wonderful reputation, and they accepted Solly. It broke her heart to leave him there, but she knew it was best. The language barrier had been broken the night Conrad Ellis was killed. Solly eventually spoke almost normally, although occasionally he would get stuck on words or phrases."

"Did he remember or ever know—"

"What he'd done? No. Mother never burdened him with the truth of that."

"Did he ever learn to read, as she'd hoped he would?"

"He did, yes. He grasped mathematical concepts that boggled most minds, and he could construct complicated models of buildings and bridges, but he was never able to direct those skills toward any vocation. Perhaps now, with advanced knowledge and understanding of autism, he could have. But the condition wasn't even given a name until the mid-forties.

"When he was too old to stay at school, Mother brought him home. He had an aide who looked after him while she worked. He was content until the day he died, suddenly and unexpectedly at age thirty-two of a heart abnormality that no one knew he had.

"We grieved, naturally. But when I couldn't be consoled, Mother reminded me that Solly had a much better life than she could have dreamed he would, and he owed it to Mr. Rainwater. He knew what would have happened to Solly if anyone suspected him of killing Conrad Ellis. He would have been dragged away and locked in an institution for the criminally insane, probably cruelly abused every day for as long as he lived. In that last shared moment, my father made Mother realize that the only way Solly could have a life was to let him make the sacrifice."

The couple were quiet for a time, then the man glanced at his watch. "We should go." He extended his hand, and the old man shook it. "It's been a fascinating afternoon. We got much more than we bargained for when we decided to stop."

The antiques dealer rounded the counter and walked them to the door, where the woman spontaneously hugged him, which pleased him greatly.

"Good-bye," she said. "It's been a pleasure."

"Likewise. Good-bye."

They had almost reached their SUV when she turned back. "Did Mr. Rainwater know about you?"

He smiled. "Dr. Kincaid was able to tell him only hours before he died. Weakened as he was, he wrote my mother a letter. She kept it with her always, on her person. She was never without it. Never without him."

Reading the question in their eyes, he shook his head. "She told me everything I've told you, but she never shared the contents of that letter. I'm sure the message was far too dear to her to be shared. She was buried with the letter along with the copy of A Farewell to Arms that he'd given her."

He looked down at the timepiece lying in his palm, then folded his fingers around it tightly. "His watch she gave to me."

About the Author

Sandra Brown is the author of seventy *New York Times* best-sellers, including *Mean Streak, Friction, Sting, Seeing Red,* and *Tailspin,* the latter two debuting at #1. Since the launch of her career in 1981, Brown has published eighty novels, most of which remain in print. Her books are translated into thirty-four languages. She lives in Arlington, Texas.